The Genesis

Ghosts

The Oliver Anderson Trilogy,
Book Two

A Biblical Paranormal Fantasy

by

Joshua David Jones

The Genesis Ghosts
The Oliver Anderson Trilogy, Book Two
© Joshua David Jones 2021
First Edition
ISBN 9798581931011

Cover and interior illustrations by Anthony DePietro of Depietrodraws.com. Cover designed by Stephen Melniszyn of Stephen Melniszyn Designs.

The Oliver Anderson Trilogy

Girl and the Guardian - The Genesis Ghosts - Samson and the Siren

(Mordecai & Esther)   –   (Judah & Tamar)   –   (Samson & Delilah)

<u>Notes to Reader</u>. First, this book is written in British English, I hope those used to American English will find the change enjoyable rather than burdensome. Secondly, this book is based on the strange happenings recorded primarily in the 38th Chapter of Genesis in the Hebrew and Christian Scriptures. I recommend examining the ancient source material itself.

<u>Thanks</u>. To Irdi Jones (my wife), Imogen Lowe, John Spencer, Abi Proudfoot, Anne Miles, and Carla van Keulen for your helpful feedback as the manuscript developed. Thanks to Anthony DePietro for the front illustration and Stephen Melniszyn for the cover design.

1

HIS CALLOUSED HAND flowed down the contours of her scented back and along her naked thigh. The titillation of the touch helped him ignore his headache.

He'd imagined caressing her like this for years, but only now was the dream made flesh. His infatuation began the first moment they'd met. Getting financially prepared to marry, however, had taken a long time.

Yesterday, they'd celebrated their wedding and last night was their first time in bed. Having longed to make love to her for so many years, he thought it ironic that his hangover now prevented him from remembering the night's details. His father-in-law had insisted he try all his best wines.

'You awake?' he asked.

'Hm,' she purred with contentment.

'How was last night for you?'

'Mm.'

His body tingled at the thought of having pleased her. 'Good, huh? I look forward to a second time—sober!' His fingers continued to dance across her back. 'Whaddya say, after breakfast, we come back here for more cuddling?'

She turned around with wide eyes and smiled. 'I'd love that!'

He swung his arm forward and slapped her in the face. Hard.

He leapt to his feet. 'What are you doing here?' he shouted at the unexpected woman. She held her face, unable to respond. His hand had never struck a woman before, but she was not his wife. 'Why are you in my bed?' he shouted.

'You hurt me!' she cried as blood poured from her lip.

'Why are you here? Where's your sister? Where's my wife?'

'I *am* your wife. You married me yesterday.'

Jacob fell back onto the pillows, naked and in shock, trying to digest her words and what they implied. 'You mean—?'

Leah nodded. 'Yes, father replaced her with me.'

'No! It can't be. I married Rachel!'

'Don't be disappointed—I'm not a bad replacement. We can make this work, right? I'll love you as much as she would've.'

A single word fumbled out of his open mouth. 'R-replaced?'

2

London, 21st Century

ELISE AND HER friends finished their last lecture and scurried out of the school. They navigated their way through the city towards their favourite coffee house—turning more than one head as they went. The group of girls were discussing their plans for the weekend when Elise's pocket buzzed. She pulled her phone out and checked the message.

She froze.

It was from Oliver. *Quick, I need your help. Can you meet me in the south car park? It's urgent!*

The words took Elise's breath away. She turned to her friends. 'Sorry, please enjoy the coffee without me. Oliver's in big trouble. See you all Monday?'

'I'll go with you,' Becca said. Elise accepted her offer and the others expressed their concern as the two rushed off.

Elise flew across the campus with Becca trailing behind. She found Oliver in the car park next to his small vehicle and ran up to him. 'Oliver! What happened? Are you OK?'

'It's this piece-of-junk car my dad advised me to get,' Oliver complained, hitting the top of his Fiat. 'It won't start. That's the third time in two months.'

Elise brushed her fair, blonde hair out of her face and gave him a quizzical look. 'Oh? Are you hurt or anything?'

'Um, no. Why?'

Becca ran up beside her friend. Panting, she looked Oliver up and down. 'He doesn't look dead to me.'

'Hello Becca,' Oliver said stiffly.

'Oliver,' Becca said with an equally formal nod of the head. 'What's the big emergency?'

'Like I was just telling Elise, it's this crappy car.'

'Wait, that's it? You had us run across campus for that? We thought it was urgent!' Becca scolded him as she put her arm around Elise.

'I wasn't asking for your help, Becca. I was asking Elise because, unlike you, she's a kind and wonderful human being. And, so that you know, this *is* an emergency.'

Becca rolled her eyes. 'I can't even! Elise, are you gonna waste more time on this man-child?'

Elise squeezed her hands in front of her and took a deep breath. 'Thank you for running all this way with me, Becca. You're a good friend,' she said gently.

Becca crossed her arms. 'Uh-oh. I hear where this is going. You're not thinking of helping him again, are you?'

'I just want to see what he needs,' Elise said gently.

'I can't allow this! You've bailed this pathetic boy out enough this year. Come on, walk with me back to the café.'

Oliver realised he needed to get rid of Becca if he was to get help from Elise.

'You know, Becca, I think I hear one of those extra-large caramel latte things calling out your name right now,' Oliver shot back, taking the verbal gloves off. 'It's saying, "Becca, come get me—me and your friend, the cake." Get to it. It'll be one of your five-a-day. You could try jogging there—assuming that running across this car park hasn't used up all your exercise ability for the month.'

Becca gritted her teeth and her eyes ignited—as if to shoot lasers into Oliver's skull. 'Why you lazy, no good excuse—'

Elise put her hand gently on Becca's shoulder. 'Please you two,' she implored.

Becca turned to Elise. 'I'm just trying to look out for you. I don't want this excuse-making, knuckle-dragging male to take advantage of you. We should walk away now!'

'Listen, cupcake, you're not her mum. Elise is perfectly capable of making her own decisions.'

'Cupcake? I'm not gonna be talked to like that by a little nobody like you,' Becca snapped back.

Oliver tensed up and prepared to fire off more word bullets.

'Guys, please!' Elise pleaded.

They paused.

'Becca,' Elise said, turning to her friend, 'Could you please give us just a minute? I'll meet you at the café.'

Becca rolled her eyes. 'Really? You're gonna do this?'

'Just for a minute, OK?'

'Uh-huh,' Becca moaned. 'OK, I'll join the girls. But don't take too long.'

'Thank you,' Elise replied as her friend walked off with indignance pulsating from her body.

Oliver watched his enemy march off, but he wasn't celebrating his victory. His mind was racing through ways he might convince Elise to help him with his plan for the night.

3

ELISE PUFFED AND turned back to Oliver. 'Cupcake? Really?'

'Huh? Oh, was that too much?' he replied, snapping back to attention.

'Beccas's not as terrible as you think.'

'OK,' Oliver yielded. 'I'll try to be more careful with my words around Miss Cupcake in the future.'

'Thank you,' She replied, trying to hold back a laugh. 'Anyway, I'm sorry about your car. How can I help?'

Oliver's defences melted at her offer of assistance. She was the kindest girl Oliver knew and possessed a sweetness that seemed to encapsulate everything he imagined femininity should be.

Oliver grinned. 'You wouldn't be spending the weekend with your family, would you?'

Elise gave a shy smile back. 'Yes, of course. I spend every weekend with them, why?'

Oliver knew she did. She'd told him before about her family and how close-knit she was with her siblings and parents. Her family bonds were something he admired about her—even if he went out of his way to avoid spending time with his own.

'They live in Guilford, right?' he asked.

Her smile grew. 'You've been paying attention.'

'Well, my filming sight isn't far from Guilford. Is there any chance I could get a lift with you?'

'Oh? Um, how far away exactly?'

'I'm not sure. I have the postcode. It's a place called "Quaker Manor", out in the country.'

'Out in the country?' Elise groaned, knowing what London traffic on the infamous M25 was like on a Friday afternoon. 'That would probably make me late for dinner.'

Oliver had already considered what a big ask this was for her. Elise's family were immigrants from the Czech Republic, and family meals bordered on the sacred.

He tilted his head down and lifted his eyes pleadingly. 'I know how important family meals are for you. I wouldn't ask unless I needed big help.'

'It's not just Friday dinner, Oliver,' Elise said softly, her eyes looking down at his feet. 'Today is the fifth of December.'

Oliver pressed his lips together to put on an understanding face. 'Yes, it's the fifth. And the fifth it is …' Oliver's mind raced for why this date might be significant. He remembered her birthday was in October. After a brief pause, he confessed. 'Sorry, I'm drawing a blank. Is that your parent's anniversary or something?'

'What? No! It's, well, in Czechia, it's an important day—it's the evening before St. Nicholas Day.'

'St. Nicholas? As in Santa Claus?'

Elise shook her head and smiled. 'It's funny how you English know so little about St. Nicholas Day. In some parts of Europe, it's huge.'

'So, do you guys eat special food? Pierogis or something?'

Elise put her hand to her mouth to keep from laughing.

'What? That's not it?'

'You're so English,' she giggled. 'It's not "pierogis". "Pierogi" is already plural. Also, that's Polish food, not Czech.'

'I know. I was just testing you,' Oliver said with a wink. Embarrassment might have overtaken others at such an error, but Oliver had the uncanny ability to charm his foot out of his mouth whenever the circumstances demanded—which was often. Still, he felt torn. He knew, if he pressed her, Elise would give him a lift, even if it meant being late for her family dinner.

He swallowed his self-hatred and pressed on. 'Elise, I know your family is important to you and I wouldn't ask unless I had no other way. For my trailer, I need to meet some lads from Wales out there to film for the night. Please, I need this.'

She felt his desperation. She wished he hadn't waited until the last minute. The school had given them two months to film and edit this trailer. Still, despite his procrastination, she cared for him. 'I'll message the girls so they know what's happening. We should go soon. I don't want to be later than necessary.'

'Really? Thank you!' Oliver smiled—though he felt dirty, knowing he'd taken advantage of her kindness. 'No need to lose out with the girls though. I need to load up your car with equipment. That'll take a few minutes—you can go say bye.'

Elise considered. 'OK. But, please, load it quickly.'

'Of course. I wouldn't want any Czech mama angry with me,' he said, flashing his smile. 'It'll take less than fifteen minutes to load up—enough time for you to grab a coffee.'

Elise loved Oliver's smile. 'Alright, I suppose we can do this.'

'Thanks, you're the best!' Oliver exclaimed, putting his hand on her shoulder, a move that shot a tingle through both of them. 'If you give me your keys, I'll drive your car around back and load it up.'

'OK,' she agreed. She pulled her key chain out of her handbag and placed it in Oliver's hand. 'Please take care of it.'

'Hey, it's me,' he grinned. 'Plus, it's just to the back of the school. No one can mess that up.'

'Alright, Oliver, I trust you,' she said, giving him a quick hug before turning to head back across the car park.

'Thanks,' Oliver said. 'Oh, Elise!'

She spun around. 'Yes?'

'When you go to the coffee house, could you get me one?'

'Sure. Black, right?'

'Yeah, thanks! I'll get it next time,' Oliver promised, remembering he'd said that the last five times.

'See you in a bit,' she said and hurried off.

'Now,' he murmured to himself as his smile faded, 'What will I put in your car—and will I tell you about it?'

4

16th Century BC

Paddan Aram, Mesopotamia

'ISN'T IT ENOUGH that we're married? That I'm the mother of your children? Why are you still obsessed with her?'

Jacob sighed. He hated these arguments. He turned his gaze towards his sons who were playing next to them. 'I've loved her since I first laid eyes on her. I've never pretended otherwise.'

Leah's lips pressed together and her neck muscles tensed with rage. Her eyes flashed fire. 'But I'm the one who's given you children. Aren't these enough for you?' she asked, holding up their baby daughter.

Jacob studied his boys. Reuben was wandering around the tent aimlessly. Simeon and Levi were wrestling again. Judah, the youngest boy, was stacking blocks. He spoke gently but truthfully. 'I love these boys. And I respect the mother you've become but, as for us, do we need to go over this again?'

'You'll be with her tonight, I suppose.'

Jacob breathed deeply and exhaled. 'Yes.'

'Like most nights.' Leah turned her head away, fighting off rejection's arrows. 'Fine, then. I'll stay here and take care of our children while you're with her.'

Jacob felt sorry for his wife, but he hated her theatrics. 'She's your sister,' he sighed. 'It's not my fault I'm married to both of you. Take your anger out on your father if you must. But don't play the victim. You went along with his deception.'

Leah bit her lip and turned her back. He was right—she often played the role of the innocent victim. But she had gone along with her father's plan. She deceived Jacob to secure her place as a wife—an act that doomed her to a loveless marriage.

Jacob took her silence as his cue to exit the tent.

After he did, Leah placed her elbows on her knees, put her hands in her face, and wept. Judah waddled over to his mama and put his palm on her arm. She looked at her boy and wrapped her hand around his. 'Judah, my energetic boy. Don't envy any of your brothers the way I did my sister. If you try to grab life too tightly, you'll choke it.'

5

OLIVER LAID AN old camera, swaddled in a blanket, on the backseat of Elise's green car. He'd always thought her vehicle was a sickly shade of green. Which is exactly how he felt at the moment: sick.

His mind was all tangled up, trying to figure out what to do. School policy stated students could take older cameras and lights off-campus for film projects. Students were not allowed, however, to take the newer equipment off the premises. They were only to be used under staff supervision.

And that's why Oliver was at war with himself. In his mind, the importance of this project justified breaking the rules. He had planned for days on taking the forbidden equipment. But, now that he needed Elise for a lift, he was in a conundrum. It was one thing for him to take the new equipment in his car. But to take it in Elise's? That was different. Elise was the most innocent girl he'd ever known. He feared what she might think of him if he went through with it and she found out.

But why not? It's not stealing. I'd just be borrowing, he reasoned within himself.

But he knew Elise wouldn't approve. *No, I'll only take the old cameras and lights,* he replied and headed back inside.

But that's when the darkness came. The muscles in his back tensed up and his breathing grew heavier. Thoughts of losing his victory from the previous year leavened his imagination and caused his heart to race. Whispers flashed through his mind: *Last year you became a somebody. Don't let yourself go back to being a nobody, a peasant.*

Oliver turned to the left and headed for the side room, driven by a force greater than himself. *OK, then … I'll simply take the new equipment for the night and have it back Saturday morning before anyone notices it's gone. No one gets hurt—so no one needs to know.*

He came back out with two new cameras, one in each hand, and placed them gently in the backseat of the vomit green car. He stood up and, perhaps out of instinct, looked around to make sure no instructor or other students were watching. *I'm not stealing,* he reassured himself. *I'm a second-year student borrowing equipment. It'll be returned in twenty-four hours.*

He soothed his conscience and prepared to head back inside when he noticed someone on the other side of the car park who had almond skin and dark features. He wore a fitted suit, sported a well-trimmed beard, and carried a small drinking glass in his hand.

And he was looking straight at him.

Oliver turned away and headed back into the school. Before he stepped through the door, he glanced back over his shoulder. The man was still looking in his direction. 'Why's he staring at me?' Oliver mumbled to himself. He rolled his shoulders back and re-entered the school. When he returned with a couple of lights, the man had left. *That's London for you.*

He made a couple more trips back and forth into the school and wrapped up the lights and cameras with blankets that would provide safety padding and, just as importantly, they'd keep Elise ignorant of what she was transporting.

Oliver had finished loading when Elise returned with the two coffees. 'Here you go, Oliver,' she said with a smile.

'You're amazing. I owe you one—or a few' he responded.

Elise smiled at his acknowledgement of his growing coffee debt. 'You ready?'

Oliver gave a curt nod. 'Yep, just finished.'

'OK, I'll drive and you give me directions,' Elise said. 'You got everything you need?'

'Yep. A few old cameras and lights—nice and secure. Extra blankets, just to be safe.'

'Good thinking. Well, if you're ready, let's get going. It'll be dark soon.'

'Yes,' Oliver said, opening the passenger door. 'I don't want you to be late for your Santa meal.'

'It's a family dinner,' she corrected with a gentle grin. 'The festive stuff begins afterwards when we put our shoes out.'

'Shoes?' he began, 'Never mind, you can explain in the car.'

They climbed in and off they went. They navigated London's busy streets toward the setting sun with the prohibited equipment snug in the back. They were both eager to make good time.

But more than just the Welsh boys planned to meet Oliver in the countryside. A group of peculiar persons also planned on meeting with him that evening. Oliver just didn't know it yet.

6

OLIVER'S TEETH RATTLED as the car bumped and banged up the gravel road. He hoped the rough journey wouldn't damage the cameras and lenses he'd carefully laid in the back.

He looked down at the map on his phone. 'I think we're almost there. The connection is rubbish, and this dirt road doesn't even appear on the map.'

'I'm sure we'll find it,' Elise said reassuringly. 'It'll just take longer now that it's dark.'

'Are there roads this bad back in the Czech Republic?'

'In Czechia, we don't have paved roads.'

Oliver's eyes widened. 'Huh? They're all dirt?'

Elise laughed. 'No, of course not. When will you understand Eastern European humour?'

'Never! British banter is better. God save the Queen!'

Elise giggled again. Oliver loved it whenever he made her laugh. 'Are these dirt roads too rough for your delicate nature?' Elise asked with a wink.

'No, not at all!' Oliver objected in defence of his masculinity. 'I just don't want the school's new equipment to get damaged.'

Oops.

There was a moment of pause in the car when they both soaked in what he'd just said.

'N-new equipment?' Elise inquired. 'What do you mean?'

Oliver's mind raced for a way to avoid answering without having to lie to her. 'I, well, I may have just put something, you know, more than just the old cameras and lights in the back. You know, a couple of small necessities for tonight.'

Elise sank. 'Small necessities? Oh, Oliver. What's in the back of my car?'

Oliver took a big swallow before answering. 'Maybe some of the—'

'The what?'

'The newer stuff?'

'Newer stuff? Like the off-limit stuff?'

This is what he'd feared. 'Don't worry. It's just a few things.'

A groan escaped from Elise's mouth and a look of sadness swept over her. 'Oliver, did you steal the school's equipment?'

'Steal? No, I wouldn't call it that. I'll have it all back tomorrow. I'm just briefly borrowing,' he said, trying to justify himself. Oliver knew he'd disappointed her. Elise took a deep breath and gripped the steering wheel.

'Please, tell me everything you've put in my car.'

Oliver fought off the desire to lie. It was pointless to be less than fully truthful with Elise at this point. 'Two 4k cameras, the 8k drone, and some new mood lights. Besides the older cameras, that is'

'I have the school's 8k drone in the back of my car?' she asked nervously.

'I-I'll take good care of it. And I'll return it before anyone knows it's missing!'

'I wish you'd told me,' Elise sighed. 'I could get in trouble for this.'

'If anyone notices that it's gone, I'll say it's my fault,' Oliver said, trying to seem responsible. 'I'll tell them you didn't know.'

Elise said nothing, keeping her eye on the road.

Oliver felt like scum. 'I'm sorry. I was wrong. I should've told you when I loaded it into your car.'

A moment of silence passed. Then Elise said, 'I accept your apology. But why?'

'Why?'

'Yes, why didn't you just take the standard field equipment?'

'Because I need this trailer to be excellent—excellent and so much more. It needs to blow people away if I'm gonna win this year.'

'But you're gifted, Oliver. You could've done without all this. Had you planned it right, you could've pulled off something amazing with the regular equipment, I'm sure of it.'

'Thanks,' Oliver said appreciatively.

'Did you do it because you're scared to lose?'

The light of her question pierced him. 'I suppose,' he sighed. 'I've been nervous ever since I heard that Max got aerial footage in his dad's helicopter and that Adam filmed at a French chateau. How can I compete with that?'

'I know Max and Adam are good, Oliver. But you're even better. You have a creative insight like no one else in the school. It's just that ... why are you waiting till now? Didn't Adam get his footage last month?'

'I suppose you're all done your trailer?' Oliver asked.

'Yes, I finished editing mine two weeks ago.'

Elise was too polite to say it out loud, but Oliver knew what she was thinking. 'OK, perhaps I've procrastinated but—'

'Oh, my!' Elise interrupted with a shout and pointed out the window. 'That can't be it, can it?'

Oliver looked. In the distance, lay an old manor.

7

THEY TURNED A corner and Elise slowed down into first gear. The high beams of the car revealed a large old house on the other hillside opposite them. Even from that distance, it was clear that the old manor had seen better days.

'Quaker Manor. Well, the website said it needed repairs.'

'Why didn't you rent one in good condition?'

'Do you think I could afford to rent one in good condition? Plus, it fits in with the whole gothic vibe I'm going for.'

Elise shook her head. 'Sorry, I didn't mean to sound negative a moment ago. I'm sure you'll still do great.'

Oliver knew she was being sincere. 'Thank you.'

The car crawled carefully through the dark towards the house. 'And don't worry about Max and Adam,' Elsie said. 'You can still make up for lost time. You can smash this project—and win the contest.'

'Thank you, I will!' Oliver said, encouraged by her confidence in him.

'Just don't smash the equipment,' Elise added with a mischievous look.

'Ha! Czech humour?'

'You're beginning to pick up on it.'

'Maybe there's hope for me yet.'

'Maybe,' she winked. 'But I wasn't joking about you doing great. You'll do fine. I'm just concerned about you getting too anxious—are you?'

'Hm, I suppose.'

'But why?'

'I dunno. Ever since last year, when the school chose my script for theatre production, the pressure has been on me. I was the first first-year student to ever have his script used for a whole school production. It gave me an aura of prestige and expectation. I guess I don't believe that I deserve it.'

The car grew silent except for the slow roll of tires over the gravel. Oliver was surprised how open he'd been. Elise looked at him sympathetically. She knew how London arts could be.

'Don't let it get to you, Oliver. Do your best. If your trailer gets accepted for this year's film project, great. If not, it's not the end of the world.'

'I suppose. It's just hard for me to accept anything but another victory.'

'It is a competitive field we're in.'

'And with guys like Max and Adam? Hmph! They'd sell their own sisters off to replace me as this year's winner!'

Elise snickered. 'Oliver! That's a terrible thing to say. Those boys aren't so bad. I know Max, he's nice.'

Oliver raised an eyebrow. 'Oh?'

Elise blushed. 'I just mean he's not a shark!'

'OK, maybe it's just me imagining things to be worse than they are.'

Then they came over the hill and drove up to the front of the house. Elise's face leaned forward into the windshield. 'I've never seen one like that in London.'

Dark moss covered the brown stones and, with a bit of visibility due to the car's high beams, it seemed that many shingles were out of place or missing from the roof.

'You sure this is Quaker Manor?'

'What else would it be?'

'Well, shouldn't there be a sign or something? It looks abandoned.'

Oliver also stared through the glass. 'It's not any prettier up close. It doesn't matter—the forlornness will give it the right feel for the video.'

Elise turned her gaze to Oliver. 'I always thought English country manors sounded charming. Now I'm not so sure.'

Elise turned off the engine and left the headlights on. She looked around for another car. 'Where are the Welsh band?'

Oliver looked at his phone. 'The Ebony Mane lads should be here by now.'

'They're called "The Ebony Mane"?'

'Hey! I'm working on a budget,' Oliver laughed. 'Plus, their sound is just what I'm going for.'

'What time did you all say?'

'We agreed on six. I'll message David. He's my contact … Just a minute. I don't seem to have much of signal.'

Oliver got out of the car and walked towards a small hill to the right of the manor. Elise got out and went to get a closer look at the house's aged door and cracked windows.

When he got to the top, Oliver tried to survey the land. He got a good look at the worn face of the house and the pine trees the lined up just outside thanks to the car headlights. In the back, the moonlight gave him just enough of a glimpse to make out what seemed to be some dilapidated stables and a vast field overgrown with weeds. Oliver wondered what had happened for it to fall into such a wretched state.

'Any luck?' Elise called.

Oliver lifted his phone towards the sky. 'Ah, I've got a small bar now,' he said as he sent the message with his thumb. 'I've asked them for an ETA,' he said and descended the small hill.

'What's its history? Who lived here?'

Oliver shrugged. 'I don't know. The website said it's from the 18th Century.'

'Wow! I bet it has a lot of stories to tell.'

'No doubt.' Oliver agreed, noting the overgrown ivy crawling up the side of the house.

He turned towards. He'd enjoyed her company, but he felt guilty for the dual sins of making her late for her family dinner and for not telling her about the equipment.

'You should get going. Please don't wait with me.'

'Will you be all right by yourself?'

'I'm fine. I'll get the cameras out of your car and set up. The band will be here soon.'

Elise looked hesitant. 'You sure?'

'You've been an enormous help in driving me out here when you didn't have—' But just then Oliver's phone buzzed. 'Ah, look,' he said, opening the message. 'The band says they got delayed getting out of Cardiff. They'll be here in about thirty minutes. See? Go on, have a wonderful weekend with your family doing the Santa thingy.'

Elise gave him a playful slap on the shoulder, 'It's St. Nicholas!'

'Same difference,' he replied with an equally playful smile. 'Look, I'll set up, have a great night filming with the Welsh lads, and then they'll drop me and the equipment back off in London tomorrow. I'll see you Monday.'

'All right. But I'll help you unload the equipment.'

'Deal,' Oliver replied. They grabbed all they could and brought the equipment to the front of the house in two trips.

'You have a key?' Elise asked

'The owner said it would be under the little statue with the fox head to the right of the door. I don't see it, do you?'

'Here's a statue of a goose.' Elise said, pointing to a bush to the left of the door.

Sure enough, a bush on the left side of the door had overgrown to the point of covering a small statue of a goose. Oliver reached down and tilted the statue. 'Yep! Here it is,' he said optimistically as he brushed off the dirt from the rusty key. He stabbed it into the lock and fiddled with it for a second or two until it turned. 'Here we go.'

The heavy oak door creaked open.

'Sure you'll be safe all alone?'

'Hey,' Oliver replied, 'It's me. Plus, you've already helped loads.'

'Promise me you'll message if you run into trouble.'

Oliver held his fingers up in a scout pledge. 'Will do.'

Elise was about to leave when she remembered something. 'Should I ask you about it?'

'About what?'

'You know, the thing?'

'Huh?'

'Last month at your Grandpa William's party, remember? You asked me to remind you.'

'Oh, that. Um, thanks. I'd forgotten.'

'Didn't you promise your grandfather?' she asked, but not in an accusing or condemning way.

Oliver looked off to the side. He felt embarrassed that he'd forgotten. 'Don't worry. I'll do it tonight. Before the band gets here—or at least during a coffee break.'

'OK, I know you'll do it for him.'

He nodded. 'Definitely. Thanks for the reminder.'

'I'll go now. My family is waiting for me.' Elise leaned forward and gave Oliver a hug that sent physical and emotional warmth coursing through his body.

'See you Monday. Message me about how tonight goes.'

'Will do,' he said as he watched her get in her car. She turned the engine on, they waved one last time, and off she drove.

Oliver watched the green car disappear behind the trees. 'Goodbye,' he whispered wistfully. He lifted two boxes of equipment and turned. He stared into the manor's dim and dusty interior and, for a moment, felt apprehensive about entering all alone. But fear of being behind Max with his dad's helicopter footage and Adam with his French sceneries returned. He tightened his grip on the blanket bundles and stepped inside.

8

THE FIRST THING Oliver checked was the electricity. He flipped the switch and exhaled relief when a light bulb lit up. He was further pleased when he touched the radiator. *Warm. At least we won't be freezing tonight.*

He turned to the right and entered the main parlour. It was old and dusty but it was the perfect set up for what he was envisioning for The Ebony Mane video. It had a chandelier, a large brick chimney built into one wall, and various pieces of Victorian furniture—including an old sofa and two armchairs.

Oliver went to work in the room setting up the lights in all the right places and making plans for where the cameras would go. Some things, of course, would have to wait until the band arrived when he could see who and what would go where.

After some time, he checked his phone. *Almost eight! Where are they?* The band's tardiness unnerved Oliver. He had waited until the last minute to do this filming, and he couldn't afford to get this evening wrong. There could be no second chances.

With the room as prepared for the band as Oliver could make it, he felt entitled to a coffee break. He headed down the hallway and into the kitchen and, after looking in a few empty cupboards, he opened one to find four mugs and half a jar of instant coffee. There was no electric kettle—only an old steel one perched on the gas stove. He turned the gas on and it clicked into flame. *Wow, it still works,* he mused, pleasantly surprised as he waited for the water to boil.

Four minutes later he was sitting on an old, dusty sofa back in the parlour holding a mug of the worst tasting java that had ever entered his mouth. *Still,* he mused, *poor coffee is better than no coffee.*

He picked up his phone—no messages. He checked his connection—no bars either. He set the coffee on the table in front of him and opened the front door in search of a signal. A cold gust blew down on him as he waved his phone in the air. 'Come on, there's got to be some signal out there,' he moaned.

Oliver stood on the porch for half a minute waving his arm, but with no success. He stared out into the cold darkness. *It's cloudier and windier than it was when I arrived,* he noticed. *Darker, less moonlight now than before.* Finally, he re-entered the warmth of the house and collapsed on the sofa. He sat down and took a sip of his coffee. It was now as tepid as it was terrible and he was too tired to go make another cup.

Other than the wind and the rattling of some old boards, the house was quiet. Oliver looked over at the window and saw nothing but his own reflection on the surface of the night. He sighed deeply. Without connection, he didn't even have the internet to distract him while he waited—he wasn't used to this level of stillness.

Then he remembered.

He set the mug back down. *My promise to my grandpa and now to Elise.* Why did he make that promise anyway? Oh yeah, the party...

A few weeks earlier, Oliver had travelled to the Scottish Highlands for his Grandpa William's seventieth birthday.

'Oliver! Good to see ye, lad! How's London treatin' ye?'

'I'm managing OK, Grandpa—still in school. Not that dad's impressed.'

'Don't ye worry about him. I heard ye did well last year with that script of yers.'

'Yes, Grandpa. Thanks in no small part to you.'

The party was delightful. Oliver spoke with distant, Scottish relatives that he hadn't seen in ages—and some that he'd never met before. Grandpa William was given ample bottles of scotch, many of which he proceeded to open immediately and pass around.

It was after a couple of these wee drams that Oliver turned to him and asked, 'What can I get you, Grandpa? I want your seventieth birthday to be really special.'

Oliver wasn't entirely sure why he said it. He'd already given his grandpa a nice, leather-bound book on fairy tales he knew he'd love. But cask strength scotch can make one do and say strange things.

'Do ye mean that, lad?'

'Of course Grandpa, anything for you.'

'Really?'

'Really.'

'Read the Bible through, cover to cover,' William responded.

It wasn't what Oliver had expected. He regretted asking, but refusing him at his party would be poor form. 'Sure, no problem,' he responded. 'I read Esther after I last visited you. It was good.'

'This will take ye a bit more effort. Readin' the whole Bible differs from just readin' Esther.'

'I'll read a bit every day. Promise.' To which Grandpa William nodded with pressed lips and raised eyebrows.

That was a month ago. He hadn't read it every day. He was averaging about one day in four. He knew he'd have trouble keeping his promise, which is why he told Elise one evening after he'd returned to London. He knew she had faith and that she'd be impressed with him if he managed to do it.

As soon as he considered reading, a debate fired off in his mind: *perhaps I need a nap instead.* For a moment, he decided to go with the nap. After all, it would be a long night—and once The Ebony Mane arrived, it would be nothing but work.

He put his head back on the old sofa and closed his eyes.

But, as he drifted off, Elise's reminder—and his promise—haunted him. After some back and forth, he sat up and opened the Bible app on his phone to the place where he had last left off in the first book of the Bible. *Genesis, good to see you again. Sorry I've been away a few days. Places to go, people to ... you know the excuse.*

Oliver loved his grandpa and he didn't want to break his promise. But he struggled to understand the point of these stories. When he read the Bible's book of Esther the year before, he had respect for the two cousins, Esther and Mordecai. They took risks and sacrificed for the good of their people. But, so far, the characters in Genesis were less than impressive. Though he wasn't a Christian, he respected his grandfather's faith and believed it could help people lead good lives. What he struggled to understand was why this first book of the Bible seemed to have so many uninspirational characters. *Noah?* A drunk. *Abraham?* A liar. *Cain?* Killed his brother.

He stared at the screen and read the first lines of the Bible chapter. *Wow Jacob! Now you're having kids with multiple women. Ha! Let me guess how that's gonna turn out for you.* Every few verses he'd look back up to the top of his phone to check on the time or see if he had connectivity.

Now that Oliver was no longer setting up the lighting equipment and cameras, he felt cold. The radiators worked, but not that well—it was still an old house. The wind blew harder than before and there were plenty of drafts in the house. He reached for the blanket that was laying on the back of the sofa. He held it in his hands for a second as he debated whether or not he wanted to put such an old, dusty rag on him. The windows rattled as the wind pressed hard against them. His body shivered and he laid the blanket over his trousers. As he finished his first chapter, his eyes lids became heavier. *Judah. What was your mother thinking? Will you end up in the same crazy mess as your dad?* He wiggled on the sofa, making himself comfortable. He reasoned that, when he finished this chapter, he'd get that nap in after all.

Then, everything was dark.

9

OLIVER OPENED HIS eyes and looked out the window, but he couldn't see a thing. *How long have I been asleep? Is the band here yet?* he wondered as he reorientated himself to the dim and dusty room.

He reached over to check his phone. He jolted awake—it had been two hours! He sat straight up. *What's going on? Where's the band?* He looked around, but he was still all alone in the parlour. He glanced at his phone again. *No messages.* He sat back against the sofa and began to think, *Whaddo I do now?*

That's when he heard the cough.

He sat straight up again a looked around. 'Hello?' he called. *Could that have been the wind?*

He sat still. *Did I imagine that?* The wind howled through the cracks in the rattling windows and walls of the old manor.

Then, like a snap in a stormy symphony, the shuffling of feet reverberated down the hallway.

Oliver thought of the band. 'Hello?' he called, louder than before.

No response.

Then, the sound of water pouring and wood creaking echoed down the corridor—something was happening in the kitchen. 'Hello?' he shouted as loud as he could.

Still no response.

Then, after a still moment, he heard a cough and a spit.

'Who's there?' He pressed his face against the windowpane. He could only discern the dim outline of a few trees in the diminished moonlight—no vehicle in sight. 'David? The Ebony Mane?'

Still no answer.

He sat still amid the wind-induced groans of the old house. As he did, scuffles, creaks, and slurps echoed down the hall from the kitchen. 'Are you the owner? My name is Oliver Anderson. The guy online who's renting from you. You've got a nice house. It's big. A bit drafty. Not that I mind—all part of the charm.'

Nothing.

Oliver's breath came in quiet shudders. *This is silly. I need to get up off the sofa and go down the hall to see who it is.* He lifted the sooty blanket from off his trousers, turned his legs, and touched his feet to the floor. That's when he heard the footsteps. Someone was coming towards him. He looked over the sofa and down the dark hallway but, as it was unlit, there was only darkness at the far end—but heavy footsteps were getting closer.

When the creaks sounded like they were about to enter the parlour, a solitary glass came into view. It floated and bobbed in the air as it approached the back of the sofa. It stilled itself mid-air. Oliver opened his mouth to say something, but no words found their way out. He rubbed his eyes and stared at the levitating glass. *This is a dream, this is a dream.*

The glass floated around the room and made its way over to one of the two armchairs that faced the sofa. Then, it came to a halt and hovered about two feet over the seat cushion. Oliver stared at it. The glass tilted and emitted a slurp.

Oliver screamed as he grabbed a pillow from the sofa and threw it. The glass swung to the side and a few golden drops splashed out and fell to the floor. The pillow made a thud and dropped a few inches, only to float just above the seat.

'Well, Mr Anderson, that's not the reception I anticipated,' a masculine voice said.

Oliver stood and spun in all directions. 'Show yourself! Where are you?' He refused to believe the glass had spoken.

The air snapped. Oliver turned back to the chair where a man now sat, holding a glass of whisky that had previously been floating by itself. He fell back down on the sofa, mouth wide, and ready to yell again.

'Please don't,' the man remarked before taking another sip from his glass. 'We won't get much accomplished if you spend all night screaming at me.' He took another sip from his glass. 'I had to go with some bourbon. The coffee here is loathsome.'

Oliver's eyes were glued to the stranger, his breath was arrested, and his insides felt as if they were circling a bathtub drain. *What is this!* he screamed on the inside.

'I see you tried some. Is it just me, or did you think so too?' The man was middle-aged, had strong shoulders, and was in good shape. He had a trimmed, dark beard, and almond skin. He wore an expensive-looking suit and sat with his legs neatly crossed and his elbows on the chair's armrest.

Oliver's mind spun with questions and he had a feeling he'd seen this man before. All he could do, however, was force out an agreeable, 'Yeah, the coffee sucks.'

The thought of running away flashed through Oliver's mind as he lifted himself a few inches off the sofa. But where would he go? Outside? It was dark. Plus, was he going to leave this strange man with all the school's equipment? *You need to protect what you've borrowed*, he told himself and lowered his body weight back down.

The man sat stoically with one hand wrapped around his glass. With the other hand, he lifted the pillow from off his lap and tossed it back onto the sofa next to Oliver. He stared at the gasping young man for a few seconds and then gave a slight smile. 'Well, Mr Anderson, I guess we should begin.'

His words added confusion to Oliver's fear. 'Begin? Who are you? Are you with the band?' he asked, already knowing the answer would be negative.

'Do I look or sound Welsh to you?' The man had an accent, but it wasn't certainly wasn't Welsh or even British. He thought it might be a Latin accent—Spanish or Italian or one of those places where words have that olive oil charm. His voice was deep, smooth, and had a commanding effect over Oliver.

Oliver's heart thumped. 'I recognise you from somewhere. Did I see your picture on the internet with this house? Are you the one I'm renting from?'

'I'm afraid not. Do I look like a man who would let his house fall into disarray? I've always taken good care of my physical property even if I've not always done so with my relationships.'

'If you're not the owner, who are you? How'd you just appear in that chair?' Then a light flashed. 'Wait ... the car park.

I saw you earlier today. What are you? Some kinda magician? A stalker?'

The man set his glass on the floor and folded his hands in front of him. 'So many questions. Let's see, first, I am a man from the past. Second, you're too ignorant to understand how I relate to space and time. Lastly, I have been stalking you today and I am, what some might call, magical. Supernatural, if you'd prefer.'

'Magical? Supernatural?'

'Something like that.'

'This is a joke them, right?'

'Is it?' the man asked.

'Am I on camera?'

'The only cameras in this room are the one's you brought.'

'Well, you need to tell me who you are,' Oliver demanded.

'I already did.'

'No, you said that you were magical—there's no such thing as magic.'

'Is there not?'

'Of course. It's the 21st Century.'

'Is it now?' the man asked. 'Explain to me, pray tell: what does that have to do with anything? Did magic stop existing before this year? Was there a particular century when it ceased to exist? Why must the new be any less magical than the old?

Oliver put his hand to his forehead. 'No,' he said with a sigh. 'Magic never existed. Look, I don't know who sent you, but you freaked me out. Congratulations. Perhaps you meant it as a joke, but this isn't funny. Plus, I'm expecting a band to arrive any minute so, whoever you are, please leave!'

The man lifted his hand and snapped his finger. Instantly, he disappeared.

Oliver's jaw dropped. 'Wha … OK that's creepy. I don't know how you did that. Hello! Hello!' Oliver's voice echoed in the parlour and through the house.

Then, like a lightning bolt, a blow struck him on the side of his face. Pain shot through his body and he fell onto the sofa.

10

OLIVER'S HANDS WRAPPED around his face. The slap had hurt, but the unexpectedness of it all is what shook him the deepest. He was in pain but, even more, he was unnerved.

'Come now, Mr Anderson. I didn't come to hurt you unnecessarily. You will suffer tonight, but that is not our goal.'

Oliver looked up in the space over the sofa. He heard the voice, but couldn't see man. Then, he heard another snap and the stranger instantly appeared again.

'No!'

'Oh, please don't yell again' the man sighed and walked back to the armchair. He looked over at Oliver, shivering on the sofa. 'Relax. I've come here to talk.'

Oliver looked up and caught his breath. 'Why—why'd you hit me? That hurt!'

'I know you're in drama school, but there's no need to overreact. It was only a slap. You were trying to throw me out because you thought I was a joke. I struck you because we need to dispense of childish notions if we're going to make any progress.'

'So, you're what then? A dream, right? A person can feel pain in a dream. So, yeah, you're not real.'

'Why can't I be both real and a dream? I've discovered dreams to be terribly real—though I didn't always think so.'

'You've got to be a dream—you can't be a ghost.'

For the first time, the stranger laughed. 'A ghost? Ha! That's rather ironic.'

His reaction puzzled Oliver. 'W-why do you say that?'

'If you let me, I'll explain why I think so later.'

'So you're not even pretending to be a ghost, right?'

'It depends. I'm dead if that's what you mean,' he responded coolly, picking up his glass for another sip.

'You're dead? Like a zombie?'

'Zombies are half dead. But, though I'm dead, I'm far more alive than you can imagine.'

'You're dead and alive? And you drink...'

'Bourbon.'

'Bourbon?'

'I suppose shall tell me I should stick to Scotch instead? Well, with a name like "Anderson" I suppose your Scottish heritage demands it. Your protesting is to be expected.'

'It doesn't matter what type—if you're dead!'

'Relax, please. Think of me as just a man for now.'

'Just a man? OK, what do I call you? You have a name?'

'Yes, call me Judah.'

'Judah?' Oliver pressed his hand into his thigh to see if he could feel the pressure—to see if this was a dream. His mind fought to make sense of the conversation he was having. *I'm asleep. Asleep or I have a brain tumour.* 'Oh God, please don't let me have a tumour,' he whispered to himself.

'I see you're having trouble with this. Don't be afraid, I'm here to help you,' the man said, as he stood up from his chair. He walked towards Oliver and stretched out his hand. For a moment, Oliver flinched, thinking he might be struck again. But then Judah's hand rested on his shoulder. It was unusually substantial—as if the man's hand was made of granite. But it wasn't cool like stones or ghosts typically are thought to be; his touch was warm. Warmth flowed from his heavy hand into Oliver's body. His breathing came back under control, and his mind calmed.

'Don't overthink it. Madness comes from overthinking that which should be simply accepted.'

Judah returned to his chair. 'Now, I was sent here to answer your questions and more.'

'Sent?' Oliver asked, no longer fearful, but still unsure of what was happening.

'Yes, your grandfather has been praying intensely for you ever since you made him that birthday promise.'

'You know Grandpa William? Did he send you?'

'I know more about you than you might think, Mr Anderson,' Judah replied calmly. 'But, no, your grandfather didn't send me. Someone else sent me in answer to his prayers.'

His words stirred Oliver's mind with questions. He believed prayers were a form of meditation, but not that they were ever *answered*. 'What do you mean exactly?'

'We'll get to that later. First, I'm here to talk to you about the questions you asked me earlier.'

'Earlier?'

'Before you fell asleep. Don't you remember?'

'Um, no. You just got here.'

'You asked me about my mother and my life.'

'Wait... y-you're him? Judah as in, *Judah*? The Judah in Genesis?'

'I was once him, yes.'

Oliver gave a sceptical grin. 'No, that's impossible. I don't know who you are or how you're doing this, but that guy, if he ever actually existed, lived over 3,000 years ago. Who are you really?'

'I'm sure you have all sorts of questions about ghosts, or dreams, or how all of this might be working, but I'm not here to indulge your curiosity, I'm here to help you. Now part of that help will be telling you about myself. You rightly pointed out that my family was dysfunctional. But not everything that starts off bent stays that way.'

'So, you're telling me that you've come here just to share your life story? Is that the line?'

'Did you say "just"? For those with ears to hear, the story of a man's life can offer more wisdom than a whole stack of books on philosophy.'

'And what if I'm not interested?'

'I didn't come to force myself on you. If you want me to leave, I will. Simply ask, I'll disappear, and by tomorrow you will have convinced yourself this conversation was only a dream.'

'Huh?'

'Should I stay or leave? You decide.'

Oliver's face contorted. 'Wait, I have a choice?'

'There's always a choice when it comes to truth.'

'I'm not sure I know what you mean.'

'Humanity doesn't merely suffer from ignorance. It suffers from wanting to stay ignorant. Ignorance can be comforting. Truth can be offensive. Now, you decide if I stay or leave. Do you want wisdom or do you want to stay in foolishness?'

The statement was almost as surreal as the one asking it. Oliver rejected belief in the supernatural but he'd assumed that, if such things were to exist, they'd just appear with no human say-so at all.

'Well?' Judah asked, though it sounded like a command.

Oliver's knee trembled. That this all might be a dream suddenly seemed secondary. *After all, a dream can teach wisdom, right?* He didn't know how to respond. He felt afraid and wanted to wake up and have this dream fade into the fog of forgetfulness. *But what if something valuable could be gained? Wouldn't that be worth it? Do I ask this hallucination to leave so I can wake up with my sanity, or do I hear his story?*

Oliver took a deep breath. 'Stay,' he utter quickly. 'Now, to be upfront, I don't believe in the supernatural. I believe prayers can help with mindfulness and whatnot. But I don't believe—'

Oliver was interrupted by Judah snorting with laughter in his chair. He placed a hand over his mouth to help maintain his stoic control, but his laughter was hard to suppress.

'What's so funny?'

'Mindfulness!' and he snorted again as he fought to keep the laughter at bay.

'You think that was funny?'

'Mr Anderson, if there's no one on the other end of the line, don't waste your time speaking on the phone. Either your Grandpa William walks with God or he's utterly insane. Your description of his faith as something respectable, but not true, is patronizing. There's more to the Universe than the cramped little existence of what you can see and touch. But, again, we'll get to that latter. For now, you simply need to choose.'

Oliver's back pressed against the sofa under the weight of Judah's words. 'I didn't mean to offend. I'm just trying to make sense of all this. Have I inhaled toxic dust from the blanket?'

'Don't play games, Mr Anderson. I've heard you say you want me to stay. Just to confirm, have I heard right?'

Oliver's mind returned to the fork in the road. Was he making the right choice?

'Yes, stay' Oliver said, half-surprised at what came out of his mouth. 'I want to hear your story.'

11

IT STARTED WITH my mother. With my grandfather's help, she pretended to be my aunt—and married my father in her place. I know, it's weird.

My mother envied her little sister's beauty and hated that she was engaged before her. She deceived father to secure her place, but it all backfired. He went ahead and married my aunt a week later, leaving my mother to live her whole life in her little sister's shadow. Had I taken the time to listen to her, and learn from her mistake, I might've avoided so much pain.

But I didn't. And because of that, I spent much of my life despising my father—and I was haunted by my brother's ghost.

I should explain more about my family first.

It was big. I had five full-blood brothers and one little sister, who I adored. I also had half-brothers. In addition to his two sister-wives, he had two other women he slept with. They were like wives, but not really. More like live-in girlfriends—but they worked for his wives. Yeah, I know—it was complicated. Even in our time, it was seen as weird. Growing up as boys, we had some great your-mum insults. The banter was how we coped with the dysfunction.

My grandfather, Isaac, had done nothing like this. Father and Uncle Esau had grown up with one father and one mother throughout their childhood. Nice and simple. Not us, no. Our dad had to have several women.

To be fair, it's not that father was a sex maniac. He hadn't intended to have all those wives, he had only wanted to marry Rachel and ended up marrying my mum by accident. Well, it was an accident on his end, but an act of deceit by my mother.

As I said, the other two were servants of Rachel and my mother, Leah. His wives forced these servant girls on him. Yeah, how often does a man's wife come home with a girl and command him to sleep with her? A man may dream about such things, but it never happens. Well, such was the hatred between my mother and Aunt Rachel that they threw these other women into father's arms in their quest to have babies and win father's heart.

Sadly, my mother never won father's affection. It didn't matter how many children she bore him. Father had been in love with Aunt Rachel from day one, and nothing could change that. Heaven knows I hated my aunt for it.

My childhood was strange but it wasn't terrible. We had plenty to eat, and I wasn't aware enough to question father's lifestyle. He was still working hard for Grandpa Laban at the time, but he shielded us from the politics and drama of that relationship. I was naïve enough to think we were one happy family! I would play and compete with my three older brothers and dote on Dinah, my little sister. She would usually come to me for protection or help when any of the other brothers were teasing or picking on her.

One day, when I was twelve and she was eight, I came in and saw her on all fours with grass in her mouth. My two older brothers, Reuben and Levi were standing on either side of her and Reuben was prodding her with a stick.

'What's going on?' I asked.

'Ju, help! They're picking on me!'

I looked up at my brothers. 'What are you doing?'

Levi let out a laugh. 'She asked us what we do when we take the sheep out to pasture, and so we thought we'd demonstrate. Here, eat some more grass little lamb!'

'Leave her alone.'

Levi crossed his arms, in an attempt to look tough. 'Turn around and leave, shorty. We're just having some fun, we're not hurting her.'

'You're annoying me. I don't wanna eat grass!' Dinah protested.

I walked up to Levi, who was two years older than me and slugged him as hard as I could. Blood exploded from his nose and he fell back onto the ground. Reuben dropped his stick and stood speechless, not sure what to do.

I took Dinah's hand. 'Come on Dinah. Don't let these fools make you eat grass ever again.'

She took my hand and leapt off the ground. 'Thanks, Ju!'

Funny enough, Levi and I became good friends after that—and my brothers never teased Dinah again. We fought sometimes. People who grow up with a few brothers get that. But I managed to hold everyone's respect.

As a child, I admired father. I saw him as a strong and good man who prayed to the Creator-God. Aunt Rachel had the idols she'd grown up with. And my mother? Well, she had a conversion experience of sorts before I was born. She worshipped the Creator-God too—at least for a while. That's what explains the meaning of my name: Praise to Yahweh! In my childhood, I was fascinated by how my father's God had no statues to represent him as all the other gods did.

But all that child-like admiration changed when I was sixteen—when Joseph was born. His birth transformed father into a new man. He spent every moment when he wasn't working with Aunt Rachel and the baby. The way he held her and the baby. I'd never seen father so happy.

Levi noticed how this bothered me.

'You're looking as sad as you are stupid! Come, everyone else is celebrating.'

I didn't respond to his teasing. 'It's father. Look at him.'

'Whaddya mean? He's happy!'

'Exactly. Look at that smile. When was the last time you saw him smile that big over you or me?'

'Huh?'

'You know how he loves Aunt Rachel more than mum?

'It's not something I enjoy thinking about but, yeah.'

'Now he'll love her children more than us too.'

I saw the fear I felt pass into Levi's eyes as the thought registered with him for the first time. 'Stop—you're freaking me out, shorty. What's your point in saying such a thing?'

'My point is that we're being replaced.'

And that's when the darkness first gripped me.

12

MY STOMACH TIGHTENED and my teeth clenched whenever father came near me after that. I loathed responding to him in this manner, but I couldn't do otherwise. Maintaining my affection for him was battle I had to forfeit. The praises I once had for father rotted into curses and loathing. I despised aunt Rachel and envied their child.

Shortly after, when Joseph was two, we left Haran where I'd grown up and moved back down south into Canaan where father was from and met my grandparents, Isaac and Rebekah, and Uncle Esau for the first time. Though we never moved in with them, they were close enough to visit. Their nearness gave me hope that my life might still be a happy one.

But then the unspeakable happened. A local leader raped my little sister. Raped! Dinah, the delight of all. She was only fifteen for Heaven's sake! What sort of monster ruins the life of a young girl for a few moments of pleasure?

I tried to comfort her. I brought her favourite food to her. I'd listen and try to cheer her with stories and jokes. But she was never the same afterwards. Her laughter was stolen.

Simeon and Levi exacted bloody revenge on everyone involved and then some. I would've supported their efforts to kill the man who raped her, but they went too far even for my rage. My brothers killed every male in the vicinity—boys and men that had nothing to do with the rape died at the end of their blade. Their excessive cruelty made a lot of enemies for us.

I was heartbroken over Dinah. My brothers' vengeance didn't make that go away. I began to turn bitter towards the Universe and loath the God of my father—how could he let all this happen? The flame of hope that I'd had of happiness in this new land disappeared. The darkness I'd felt after the birth of Joseph flooded me in deeper ways. I went from being a bright and outgoing youth to a dark and moody young man.

I put my anger to work in the family trade. We were ranchers and sheepherders, and our wealth grew into vast amounts of livestock. People from all over Canaan bought cattle and sheep from us. Our family had always been well off, but we soon became rich. I worked harder than any of my brothers in those years.

I wanted to prove I was capable and deserved to take over the family business one day. Normally, the oldest brother takes over from the father. But the most senior, Reuben, disgraced the family by acting perversely. At eighteen-years-old, Reuben slept with Bilhah, Aunt Rachel's maidservant—the young woman she had given to father to produce children through. Whether he forced her or seduced her, I don't know. But to sleep with a woman your father has slept with is detestable to us. Father never touched Bilhah after that. He made clear that Reuben had lost the right of the firstborn.

Simeon and Levi, the next two oldest, also fell out of favour for the excessive revenge they wrought on innocent men for Dinah's rape. Their actions caused them to be passed over as well. I was next in line. I still remember the day I found out...

'Well, it would seem our heroics didn't go down well with father.' Levi muttered.

'Heroics? You killed old men and boys,' I said, not hiding the disdain in my voice. 'You soiled our family name.'

'He raped our sister! I know you care about her as much as any of us.'

'*He* is the keyword. Not *they*. If you had just gone after him, I would've happily clubbed the bastard's head with you. But you couldn't stop at just one, could you?'

'The more the merrier, I say,' Levi quipped with a cold smile.

'You've got quite a sickness in that head of yours, brother.'

'Only one?' Levi laughed. 'Come on, we were rightfully angry.'

'Your anger got the better of you. Still, had it been left to father, he probably would've done nothing. I don't know which is worse: your cruelty or his passivity.'

He spat on the ground. 'We couldn't let this go unavenged.'

'I respect you for doing something rather than nothing.'

'Speaking of respect, this makes you the next in line.'

I grinned. 'What a family, eh? Where else can the fourth born ever hope to get the honour of the firstborn?'

Levi gave me a mock salute. 'You're welcome.'

'Yeah, thanks for being a hot-head.'

'Careful,' Levi said, 'If Reuben, Simeon, and I can blow it, you're bound to screw it up at some point.'

'Thanks for the vote of confidence. When I take over, you're gonna be the dishwasher.'

Levi laughed. 'Your mum's gonna be the dishwasher.'

'How many times do I have to explain this to you? Your-mum jokes don't work with me—we have the same mum!'

In those years, I proved my worth and father trusted me. He gave me responsibility for much of the family business, and it prospered under my hand. I didn't go back to loving father. He would never love me; not like Joseph. His affection was out of reach, but I commanded his respect.

I dreamt of being a more competent and more successful man than he ever was. I wouldn't repeat his mistakes. He would be an average father in the shadow of an illustrious son. In his elderly days, frailty would force him to depend on my care and provision. His neediness for me would be the revenge I'd have for the love he withheld.

But then those dreams of family leadership also fell apart. He was planning to give that to Joseph too! I came home from doing business in a nearby village, and there he was. Father had his arm wrapped around him and he was explaining the ins and outs of our work. Joseph was only a teenager, and yet father already had plans to replace me with him! The thought of him standing as head of the family with me as one of his workers.

I'd worked for this honour. It was mine! Who was father to deny me what custom demanded? Who would I be without the right of the firstborn? I no longer sought to be loved. Men may crave affection at times, but they need honour! That's a non-negotiable. I'd laboured and kept my nose clean—clean enough anyway. Father should've been celebrating me. Me! Now he was planning on putting that boy in charge and all because he loved that wench, Rachel, more than my mother.

Father even made him a unique robe for his seventeenth birthday. He crafted it with expensive dyes. In our time, such a garment was the property of princes. The robe sickened me as every colourful stripe declared Joseph's favour and my dismissal. Those colours snuck into my dreams. I'd wake up, sweating and terrified of being a nobody.

My anger wasn't directed at Joseph. Not really. Joseph wasn't a hard worker, but he was clever and he could organise his responsibilities well enough. Up to that point, I'd done right by my little half-brother. It wasn't Joseph's fault that our father played favourites. I looked out for all my little siblings, but it was harder with him. There were moments when envy tempted me to punch the little guy. Still, I refrained.

But then Joseph's dreams came and my self-control crumbled. He started having dreams of grandeur. He spoke openly about a night-vision in which we bowed down to him as if he were a king. It got so extreme that even father corrected Joseph. What I felt then was beyond anger or resentment.

And that's when I knew I had to kill him.

13

OLIVER'S EYES BULGED. 'If you confess to a murder, then I'll be forced to call the police.'

'Does this mean you think I'm no longer an illness, Mr Anderson? It would be amusing if the police showed up only to find you accusing a figment of your imagination.'

'I-I rule nothing out!' Oliver declared, realising he still had no idea what Judah was. Still, if you killed your brother, you're a dangerous ... imagination!'

Judah raised an eyebrow.

'OK, that was dumb. But, still, did you kill him?'

'You want me to continue with the story?'

'Well,' Oliver picked up his phone, 'Yes, but it's late. I, I need to get in touch with the band first,' Oliver stuttered.

'You'd check your phone again rather than hear my confession?'

'If you are some sort of spirit, then you'd know why this project is important to me,' Oliver said, opening various apps to see if he had received a message through any of them. 'I need to win. I need to, or—'

'Or what?'

'Or one of them will take my place!'

'Hm.' Judah narrowed his eyes. 'And what would you do to keep your place?'

Oliver swung his arms wide in frustration. 'Anything!'

'Anything? I know the feeling.'

'Huh?' Oliver paused. 'What's that supposed to mean?'

'What do you think it means?'

Oliver hurtled himself off the sofa and into the middle of the room, defiant. 'Why you sick little... sickness! You can't compare my situation to yours.'

'Why not?' Judah asked, cool as ever.

'You killed your brother, I just want to win! I'm not doing anything wrong.'

'And this equipment you're using? Is it yours?'

Judah's question caught Oliver off guard. 'Wait! That's not the same. I'm just borrowing stuff—no one gets hurt!'

'Humanity's ability to bend morality to get what it desires is one of its more remarkable, and unfortunate, traits,' Judah commented, casually looking at his nails. 'If you win by cheating, won't that hurt those you're competing against? Someone else might otherwise win—and gain the privileges that come with such a victory.'

Oliver knew Judah had a point. He wasn't, however, prepared to concede the argument that easily. 'There's a world of difference between coming in second place and being murdered. Yes, I am slightly bending the rules. But I need this. Winning two years in a row will guarantee me an internship in any studio in London and maybe even a job.'

'Whatever it takes to secure your place in life, eh?'

'No. I'm not saying that. There are limits to what rules you can break. We just need to use common sense.'

'Rules about rules? And who decides which ones we can break? You? Me? The Russian mafia? Let me ask you, how would you feel if you had abided by all the rules and lost—and found out later that someone else had bent the rules and won. Would you protest his victory? Or would you accept it as a fine use of "common sense"?'

Oliver clenched his jaw. He didn't want to admit Judah was right. 'I won't take an ethics lecture from a dream or a brain tumour, a hallucination, or a—'

'A ghost?'

'Whatever you are, you murdered your brother.'

'I haven't finished the story but, yes, my actions were evil.'

'Then why'd you do it?'

'Because the thought of being replaced made my guts turn inside out and haunted my sleep. I think you know the feeling.'

'You don't know me! You're a brain sickness who's messing with my mind!' Oliver stood shouted.

Judah also stood, and walked closer to him. 'Do I not? You experienced this replacement when you were fourteen when a girl you dated turned her attention to another boy—one you thought was a friend. You saw them holding hands, and you knew someone else had taken your place.'

'Shut up!' Oliver screamed and collapsed back onto the sofa.

'It happened two years later when the community playhouse gave the role you thought was yours to someone else. You refused to see the play because you knew it'd be too painful.'

Oliver clutched a sofa cushion and squeezed his eyes shut, hoping it would make Judah go away. 'All teenagers go through stuff like that. We don't carry these things into adulthood.'

'To the contrary. The fear that someone will replace you is stronger now than ever before. It's what makes your heart beat faster when you see Max and Adam speaking about their film ideas. It's what causes your jaw to clench when you see a guy at school flirt with Elise. You're afraid your little brother, who just got accepted for an engineering degree, will be your father's favourite as he's expressed disapproval of you pursuing a career in film.'

'Shut up!'

'I'm not here to judge, Oliver. Your fear was once my fear.'

Oliver let out a gasp like a man who has too long been underwater. 'No! I-I, I don't know how you know all this—'

'Nevermind that now. Just answer me: am I right? Do you know this fear?'

'I-I think … yes,' he sniffed in a tone of surrender.

'That's better. Now, tell me, how did fear drive you to steal this equipment.'

'Well, I suppose winning last year was such an unexpected joy. You know, people looked at me with admiration. I'd never had that before. Even my dad put his criticism on the shelf for a few months. I guess now I'm afraid to lose it. That's why I bor-um, stole, yes, stole the school's new equipment.'

'Now we're getting somewhere.'

Oliver stared at the floor. 'When I won last year, I felt like a somebody—perhaps for the first time in my life. So I pretended I was. But now the contest has come again and I must face the truth I've tried to avoid: last year's victory was a fluke. It's not just because I'm lazy. I've put off this project because I feel insufficient.'

Judah nodded his head. 'Is this the first time you've felt this way?'

'No, it's been the story of my life. I put off trying new things because I fear I wouldn't be good enough. So I don't try. That's why my dating life is weak. I've relied on an app on my phone to hook me up with strangers because dating means someone gets to know me. Once they do, they'll see who I am and leave. Even if I try my best, I'm not enough. Someone else will win.'

Judah looked at him sympathetically. 'And your father?'

Oliver looked up and met his gaze. 'Yes, growing up I did have that. It's only since I studied film that's he's disapproved. I'm happy my brother got into engineering school, but there's an edge to it. My dad sees engineering as a real job and my choice as a mistake.'

Judah sighed. 'I gave up on my father's love. But later, when he replaced me with my little brother, that's when I snapped.'

'I guess I can understand how you felt. I mean, here I am with the school's equipment—stolen.' he managed to admit.

Judah walked back to his chair and sat down. 'The fear of being replaced makes you do what you thought you'd never do.'

'But murder? How can you live with yourself?'

'There's more. Do you want to hear it.'

Oliver looked at his phone. It was near ten o'clock and he had no message from the band. 'Yes, I do. But … I'm not sure.

Perhaps I should go out searching for the band. I must do this filming tonight.'

'Must you?'

Oliver hesitated. 'I suppose, if this is just a dream or hallucination, then there is no point. Hopefully, they'll wake me or bring me to back to consciousness when they arrive.'

'You're choice: do I continue or not?'

Oliver looked at his phone and then at Judah. 'Ye-yes,' he managed to decide. 'Please, continue. What happened with you and your brother?'

14

I DIDN'T HAVE to find an opportunity to murder Joseph. The opportunity found me. A group of us brothers were looking after the flocks near Dothan. It was the usual: herd them to grass, make sure they get water, and don't let them wander off. Being a Londoner, you've probably never seen shepherding up close. It's not as easy as you urbanites suppose. Moving hundreds of sheep, all of whom have different ideas about where they should go, isn't easy.

Not that most of my brothers or I minded hard work. There was money in those big, dumb animals. We cared for them in the day and then ate and drank in the evening around the fire. The banter was good and we got along more times than not. But sometimes the conversation turned dark. Father had become less subtle regarding his intentions about Joseph.

Everyone saw it. But we'd only recently dared to discuss it openly.

One evening, I sat down near the fire after finding a lost sheep. Most of my brothers had begun to eat already.

'Well roasted, Levi. You didn't screw dinner up too badly this time. Tender. The stupider an animal is, the better it tastes.'

Levi didn't miss a beat. 'You'd be delicious then, Dan.'

'Your mum!' Dan replied.

Simeon jumped in. 'At least his mum can cook!'

'Lads! We've had a good day. Let's not get into mum insults. Respect the matriarchs,' Reuben said, attempting to be a leader.

'Respect the living ones, anyway,' I sneered.

Murmurs ran through the darkness. Rachel had died not long before in childbirth. The woman who'd kept our father from loving any of our mothers was gone. But not before bequeathing a second son into the world. There was now a toddler in the camp—one we feared would be Joseph 2.0.

Naphtali pressed the conversation further into the darkness. 'Do you ever think about the future of all these herds?'

'What good will it do to bring that up, Naph?' Reuben asked.

'You guys know what I mean,' Naphtali continued, ignoring Reuben. 'Who are all these herds gonna belong to? Will they be yours, Dan?'

'Nope.'

'Yours, Levi?'

'Not mine, Naph.'

'Will they belong to anyone here?'

Silence. We feared the answer to this question. Had our father planned to hand over the headship of the family to any of us there, it would've been tolerable. We could work for a respected older brother who'd proven himself. But now it seemed inevitable we'd all be beholden to the brat who made our lives miserable.

'Joseph!' someone finally shouted.

'I'm not working for that twat!' cried another.

'Nor I. If he wants the family business, he can herd all these sheep himself.'

'Where's he at, anyway?'

'Back home in the tents, feasting with father while we do all the hard work.'

'Damn him.'

'Guys, he's our brother—' Reuben began so weakly I wondered if even he believed it.

'He's our half-brother,' I corrected.

'We're all half-brothers,' Reuben countered.

'But Joseph is different.'

Joseph was clever, but he could be lazy. The image of us labouring under his leadership, eating at his table, and living off his generosity made us sick.

'It should be you, Judah,' Asher said. Reuben, Simeon, and Levi didn't object.

'I wouldn't have minded working under your leadership, Judah. You've always done right by us. You're the first one out in the fields each morning and the last one back in each night.'

'Thanks, fellas,' I replied with a nod.

'That used to be the plan, right?'

'Father had a change of mind,' I muttered, as much to myself as to the group.

There was silence around the fire. Then Levi's voice rose above the crackling wood. 'What if there was an accident?'

'Whaddya mean, accident?' Reuben objected. More silence followed. We knew exactly what Levi's question implied—and the idea grew like an ink stain in our imaginations.

Asher broke the silence. 'Accidents happen all the time here in Canaan's wilderness.'

'Someone could fall from a cliff.'

'Wild animals or bandits might attack.'

'Guys, stop it! We're not having this conversation,' Reuben said in exasperation before he stood up and walked to his tent.

'Lightning strikes people on the mountains sometimes,' Dan said, followed by a group chuckle. The conversation died down after that. It was late and we'd been drinking strong beer from Ur. It was just late-night talk. Right?

15

THE NEXT MORNING, I got up early to check the flocks. My brothers were up soon after and we prepared ourselves to move to another valley. Once the tents were packed up and the sheep were in tight formation, Zebulun pointed, 'Look!'

We all gazed into the distance. 'What is it, Zeb?'

'Don't you see who's coming?' he replied.

'I see nothing.'

'There! On the third hill to the left.'

'Your young eyes must be sharp. Screw getting old!'

'Can't you see the colours?'

And then, one by one, we saw it. Like a peacock wandering towards us, there was the robe. We knew it—and we hated it.

'What's he doing wandering out here?'

'Don't you remember when he came out to "visit" us at Shechem?' Simeon asked.

'We were naïve enough to think he was being friendly.'

'I wasn't.'

'Says you now.'

'He reported to father about the girls we hired.'

'Those girls were good.'

'Shechem girls are the best.'

'Father didn't care how fine they were. He yelled at us and forbade wine at the dinner table for a week.'

'I remember that—a week without wine. Miserable!'

'So, father sends our little brother out to supervise us.'

'It's like he's trying to insult us.'

'Maybe Joseph has another dream to share with us.'

'He can take those dreams and shove 'em up his arse.'

Finally, I asked what no one else was brave enough to ask. 'What will we do now that he's here?'

No one responded.

I asked again. 'Are we nothing but talk?'

The question hung in the air. The conversation from the night before surged back into our minds.

'There are some vicious animals out here,' Levi quipped.

'Guys, no!' Reuben protested.

'It would be a shame if any animals found him—foolish of father to send him this far by himself,' Levi added.

'Stop this!' Reuben continued. 'Yes, he's obnoxious. But we can't murder our brother!'

'Reub, you wanker—this is our only option!' Levi shouted, setting off a chorus of voices eager to debate the issue.

I raised my hand, and the noise died down. 'We can't leave things as they are, Reub. Spending our lives subservient to Joseph is not an option we can tolerate. Be reasonable.'

'Is murder "reasonable"? No! I won't let you kill our brother,' Reuben fired back.

It wasn't a power struggle. Not really. Reuben was the oldest, but he didn't have the respect of the brothers. 'He's our half-brother, Reub. He's the son of a woman who made our mothers miserable. Is that someone you want to serve?'

'I ain't serving him,' Asher said, spitting on the ground.

'Nor I,' many others echoed.

The look of defeat was already on Reuben's face. I offered a concession—both to him and to any of the brothers who felt hesitant. 'You know the dry well on the other side of the hill? Let's throw him in there. How's that for a compromise? We'll toss him in, then we can decide what to do. OK?'

I called it a compromise, but anyone thinking knew where this would end. Reuben had no choice but to accept my offer. 'Fine! Put him in the pit. But no killing him!' he declared—as if he was in charge.

'Of course,' I replied with a mock bow. He thought we were just hungover. He imagined that, when we all calmed down, he could send Joseph home. He didn't understand how long I'd been contemplating getting rid of him. None of them did.

The deed was a whirlwind. When Joseph approached, I greeted him. Seconds later, the others grabbed him. We didn't use rope. No need to tie him. The well was deep enough to keep him in.

At first, none of us regretted it. Our hearts raced at the sight of our broken enemy. It was the initial thrill of revenge.

At first, he cursed us in his anger and arrogance.

'Father will kill you if you hurt me. Idiots!' he squealed as we dragged him to the pit. We only laughed.

But, as the hours passed, his tone changed.

'Guys, I'm sorry! Whatever I did, I'm sorry! Please, let me out. I won't tell father, I promise!'

It irritated all of us. Reuben and a few others took some sheep and went exploring for fresh grass to escape his the sound of his pleas. Yes, it was callous. But, at the time, it seemed like the only course. Our futures and fortunes were in jeopardy.

His cries wore on us and I knew it couldn't continue for long. After trying to ignoring him, I finally grabbed a stone and walked to the pit. The brothers saw, but no one stopped me.

I got to the edge and shouted, 'This will teach you to shut up you spoiled brat. I'll put a hole through your dreams with—'

But I didn't finish my sentence. Off in the distance, an image caught my eye. It was a trader's caravan. That was nothing unusual. But, this time, an idea erupted into my imagination. *Why kill my brother for nothing when I could have someone else kill him and get money for it?*

I turned to my brothers and shared my thoughts. We agreed. Two of them ran to the caravan. Two of us lowered a rope to Joseph. Stupid kid. He thought we were setting him free.

We sold him to the traders for twenty pieces of silver. We reasoned that they'd sell him to Egyptians, who'd work the lazy little prince to death. He yelled and pleaded as the traders put chains on him and took him away. We had no mercy. Envy allows for none. His shouts called out for a compassion that had long since departed—if it was ever there. We turned our backs, sat down, and discussed what to do with the money.

When Reuben returned, he acted appalled. He got in my face and told me off. It confirmed my assumption that Reuben had hoped to set the boy free—perhaps to use the whole episode as an attempt to get back into father's good graces. I let him rant— then I shook my head, and walked away.

We devised a way to tell father. Naphtali had an idea and we agreed it was good. We tore his robe and dipped it in goat blood. We brought the evidence to our father.

I was the one who delivered the robe. The others feared father too much, but it wasn't difficult for me. I wanted to see his heart break. This was for my mother, for my sister, Dinah, and me. He'd ruined lives with his foolishness. Now he'd reap what he'd sown.

I entered his tent as my brothers stood outside.

'Does this look familiar? Do you know who it belongs to?' I asked with a well-rehearsed tremble in my bottom lip.

Those actors in your film school would've been impressed. I placed the rag into his hand and my skin touched his. It was exhilarating! I stared into his eyes and saw the waves of shock and pain shoot through him in quick succession.

He gasped, and broken sentences gushed out uncontrollably.

'It is, it's my, my son's. An animal, my son! A vicious animal. It's devoured... my son, devoured!'

Then he collapsed back on his seat like a sack of human gelatin, and I left the tent.

16

'YOU LET FOREIGNERS murder your brother and then broke your father's heart. Is that it?'

'You are correct, Mr Anderson.'

'I knew brain tumours were bad, but meeting you has redefined my understanding of how despicable they can be.'

'Yes, it was evil.'

'When the doctor cuts you out of my head, I will stab you with a rusty fork, soak you in petrol, and chuck you in the fire.'

'It would be better than I deserve.'

'So, you don't deny that you're the filthiest scum humanity's ever produced.'

'I make no justification for myself.'

'Good. You shouldn't!'

'Shall I continue?'

'There's more? Sounds like you already did your worst.'

'Yes, there's more.'

'What makes you think I'm interested? If I'm gonna hallucinate, why not something nice? Why can't I have deluded visions of Finnish bikini models? Why a bearded sociopath?'

'You must hear the rest of my story.'

'I don't want to hear! Go away.' Oliver grabbed his blanket. 'I'm gonna lie down and sleep. When I wake up again, I want you gone and a Welsh emo band to be here in your place. If you're a dream, never come back. If you're a cancer, I'll have them carve you out like a Christmas goose. We're done!'

Judah sipped his bourbon. 'You must learn from my failures so that you don't walk down the path I did.'

Oliver threw the blanket to the ground. 'I'll never do what you did. I'm nothing like you. I'd never kill my brother or lie to my dad!'

Then Judah did something that surprised Oliver: he clapped.

'Bravo! Your performance is excellent. The virtue signalling is stellar. I've rarely seen a better drama queen. Spend more time in front of the camera than behind it—you're gifted.'

Oliver's muscles tensed and his face turned red. 'You're accusing me of acting? You don't know me!' he objected.

'You've never lied to your father? Really? What did you tell him on the phone three weeks ago? What did you say when he asked you about coming home for the weekend? You told him that you were busy filming when the truth was you were avoiding him. You spent the weekend binging an action series online.'

'What? No! That's different. How do you know about that?'

'Everyone thinks their lie is different.'

Oliver paused as his mind brewed up an excuse. 'I-I didn't go home because my dad tries to talk me into changing my education when I do.'

'So, instead of telling him the truth, you lied.'

'I don't see how this is your business.'

'If I'm a malignant growth in your head, then your business is my business. If I'm something more, something you're not willing to consider—then people are my business.'

'The living are the business of the dead? I'm supposed to believe that?'

'I'm dead physically—that is, my soul is separated from my body. But you're dead spiritually because you're controlled by your vices.'

'You're one to talk.'

'Yes, I am. Because I was even deader in darkness than you. But you're on the same road I was on. Don't go where I went. I rejected true manhood for the life of a coward.'

'You think I'm rejecting manhood? What's that even mean? I won't let a ghost who killed his brother lecture me. How'd you live with your father after such a colossal lie?'

'I couldn't and I didn't.'

'You told him the truth?'

'No. I ran.'

'Ran? Like, away from home?'

Judah sighed and sat back down in the armchair. 'Father mourned Joseph's death. The family tried to comfort him, but he'd have none of it. He became a grief addict. At first, I didn't mind. I figured the bum deserved it. But, as the weeks and months passed, it became unbearable. All the brothers felt the horror of it, but I knew the bulk of the responsibility was mine. Father's strength left him—and we had to run the family business by ourselves.'

'Isn't that what you wanted?'

'Not like this. I wanted to inherit leadership because father thought I was worthy—not because he was busy weeping for the lost son he preferred. I hated him for his grief, but I wasn't strong enough to bear my responsibility for it. I started having dreams of my brother screaming for help. The guilt a serpent squirming in my gut. I couldn't get it out and I couldn't pretend to ignore it. I found myself longing for a reckless solitude without an emotionally crippled father to weigh me down. So I left.'

'Where'd you go?'

'Not far. But far enough. I loaded up some donkeys and travelled two days south-west to Adullam where I knew a man named Hiram. We were on friendly terms. That's where my second life began—if "life" is the right term for such pain.'

'How long were you there for?'

'Twenty years.'

'Wow, a lot of years to be away. Were they as you expected?'

'I had planned on becoming a different person. I figured that, since I was living with Canaanites near a city, I'd be free to enjoy myself. I'd be my own man apart from father. None of his rules, his worship, or his rejection.'

'Did the dreams about Joseph stop?'

'Yes, they left me. The darkness lifted and I prospered. My flocks and herds grew. The first year I was there, I married— something that was a bit overdue.'

'Was your father at your wedding?'

'My family didn't know. I didn't even send word to Levi. But they heard. I was in a new place, looking for a wife, and I chose a Canaanite—something father would never approve of. It happened quickly. One day I saw this fine-looking girl. She was the daughter of a neighbour, seventeen years old, and still unmarried. I approached her father, flashed some money, met the girl, and we made the deal. She only cost five goats—much less than what the men in my family were used to paying.'

'How romantic.'

'She was soon pregnant with our first son, Er. Then came Onan less than two years later. Shelah came not long after that. Life was good: three sons, married, and a growing business.'

Oliver wasn't impressed. 'So, you murdered your brother, lied to your dad, and then went about your merry way while he mourned? You just forgot your family?'

'No, not entirely. Levi visited often. Others, on occasion. Father, thanks to me, was just the shell of the man he once was. The guilt was more than I could bear, but I didn't cut myself off. I saw him at least once a year, but I couldn't be close to him. Not if I wanted peace.'

'No rest for the wicked, huh? And you're here to lecture me about my moral failings?'

'It didn't stay that way,' Judah retorted. 'The peace I found down near Adullam, it wasn't permanent.'

'Oh? Did you lose a few sheep? A bad business deal?' Oliver asked, oozing sarcasm. 'Did your retirement fund not perform well? You poor sociopath. Can I make you hot cocoa?'

Judah responded in perfect seriousness. 'Joseph's ghost came to haunt me.'

Oliver's face twisted. 'Huh?'

'He returned when my eldest son, Er, married a local girl.'

'How?' Oliver asked, cautiously. 'He haunted you? Like, in your dreams?'

'My brother's ghost came through my new daughter-in-law.'

Judah's response puzzled Oliver. 'How's that work?'

'Er was only 17 when he started talking about this girl, Tamar, that he'd fallen for her. Er was his mother's son—fully Canaanite in the way he saw the world. He worshipped her gods and had her morals. How could I object? I wasn't exactly raising my boys in a Hebrew environment. Why should it surprise me he'd pick a wife based on the same criteria that I did when I first moved to Adullam?'

'Which was ...'

Judah sipped his bourbon. 'She was hot.'

'Well, yes. There's always that.'

'Yes, Tamar knew how to turn heads. I didn't mind having another delicious-looking female around the place, but my concern was her motives. Her family was poor, you see.'

'You thought she was a gold-digger?'

'Precisely. It was only after the engagement had become official that I found out Er had told her all about his grandpa. That was something I rarely talked about, even with my boys.'

'Wait, I don't understand. How did your dad play into this?'

'Even though I'd distanced myself from father, I was back in line to inherit the family fortune now that Joseph was gone. I didn't talk about it much, because I didn't enjoy giving the impression that I needed his money. As my oldest son, Er was then in line to inherit everything after me.'

Oliver paused for a moment to make sure he understood. 'So, this girl knew Er was set to inherit everything from his grandpa?'

'Yes, she knew. By marrying my oldest, she was setting herself up to be the matriarch over a massive inheritance.'

'Got to look out for girls like that. They flaunt their bums and boobs about to succeed in life. What did you do about her? Did you talk Er out of marrying her?'

'No, they married.'

'Oh.'

'But this is what led to the ghost and my second murder attempt.'

Oliver's eyes popped. 'A ghost *and* another murder? Who this time?'

'My son's wife.'

'You killed the gold-digger?'

'She was channelling my brother's ghost.'

Oliver shook his head. 'You killed your son's wife—'

'It's a story unto itself—'

'You killed her simply because you had nightmares about your brother?'

'There's more to it than that.'

'Don't tell me! I don't want to hear anymore. I'll just be sharing in your guilt.'

'It's only because my son died.'

'Wait, what? Your son died? How?'

'A wild animal.'

'Oh.' Oliver suddenly felt bad for the older man. 'I'm sorry.'

'Thank you. It was tragic.'

'But how is murdering his widow the answer? Maybe she did marry into your family for money—but murder?'

'It petrified me. I thought I'd put distance between myself and my sins. But they came back to haunt me—and it was more than I could bear. It was as if she'd brought a curse from Joseph into my life and I couldn't live with the torment. That's why I got rid of her,' Judah sighed. He gazed at Oliver. 'But this brings us back to you, Mr Anderson. Your desperation to have your trailer win the competition has already caused you to lie and steal.'

That pushed away every bit of sympathy Oliver felt towards Judah. 'Stop! I'm sick of this. Don't make this about me. You're the murderer here! If you need to confess so your damned soul can find peace, or however it works for ghosts, do it. But leave me out.'

'We need to talk about you. This is why I brought you here.'

Oliver's face contorted. 'What? You didn't bring me here! I'm here to film the band.'

'I'm afraid you can wait in this house forever but The Ebony Mane will never arrive.'

'What? How do you—'

'The band is three miles south of here. They're at the correct house. You are not.'

'Wha … No!' Oliver exclaimed in disbelief.

'I'm afraid it's true.'

Oliver resisted the idea, but it made sense. The unmarked dirt road, the band not showing, the key under the goose statue instead of the fox. 'Where?' Oliver shouted, rising to his feet.

'I told you, three miles south of here. In that direction,' Judah said, pointing out a window.

Oliver followed the line of his finger. He felt the dizziness of anxiety that comes with being late for an important engagement like a wedding, a doctor's visit, or the deadline for claiming a winning lottery ticket. 'Why didn't you tell me this at first?'

'You didn't ask.'

'You know all about me! If I don't get this footage, I can't win!' Oliver shouted, putting his shoes on.

'They sent me to you for a reason far more important than this contest.'

Oliver gritted his teeth. 'You understand nothing! This is my life. If I win a second year in a row, it'll set me up for success. I'll spend all of my third year picking from among the top internship programs—maybe even a paying job.'

'And this is worth cheating to get?'

'I would drown a kitten in a bowl of milk with my own hands to win this! No one will take my place!'

'You are far more like me than you know. Stay. It is cold and dark. Three miles is no short distance in such weather.'

'It's nothing when you want it bad enough,' Oliver said, as he put a single camera into his backpack. He knew he'd need the guys to drive back here to get the rest.

Judah stood. 'Reconsider. Things may become more difficult if you leave.'

Oliver looked at Judah in disgust. 'More difficult than hearing a hallucination, or whatever you are, compare his murder and deceit to my imperfections? Gee, that's a tough choice! You or the band? Hm, good-bye!'

With that, Oliver stepped out into the cold and windy night. He slammed the door, leaving Judah there with his bourbon.

He sipped and sighed. 'Ciao for now, Mr Anderson.'

17

OLIVER GRASPED HIS backpack's strap as he walked south—the wind pushing him forward into the darkness. He was only five minutes from the manor when he realised how difficult this three-mile journey might be. He was using the flashlight on his phone which, though it allowed him to see a few feet in front of him, didn't enable him to see far enough ahead to ensure he was walking in a straight line.

He zipped his jacket up to his chin. *What am I doing?* Though eager to meet up with the band, his mind was spinning to make sense of what he'd experienced. *It must've been a hallucination.* But then a thought slapped him in the face: *if that was a hallucination, why am I taking directions from it? How would a hallucination know where the band is?*

He turned and shone his phone in the direction he had come from, but he could only see a few feet away. *What if there's no house south of here? What if I can't find my way back?* The thought was a stone in his stomach.

He laid his fear aside and pressed forward, uphill. 'I need this footage no matter what,' he muttered into the wind as he marched. Already, the wet terrain had soaked through his shoes and into his socks.

A moment later, as he was descending the hill, Oliver slipped and fell in the tall wet grass, banging his head on a firm piece of turf. When he stood, he wasn't sure what direction he should walk in. The icy wind picked up and cut through his thin city jacket. *If I get lost, can I survive in these hills?* His heart rate increased. He regretted having left the house under-dressed. *It's not London. Where are the street lights and buses?* And he cursed the countryside with every profanity he could think of.

As he pressed on, the experience at the manor hovered in his mind. He disregarded the complex issue of what Judah might be and considered his life-story. Replaying it in his mind caused him to feel Judah's fear of being replaced all over again. He hated relating so easily to the motives of a murderer—even if Judah was just the outworkings of his tired mind.

As Oliver mused over his fears, he saw a light. It was far off, but he headed for it. *Maybe that's the real manor.* His phone told him he'd only walked for twenty minutes. *Not long enough to be three miles. Well, maybe they'll direct me or give me a lift.* Just imagining himself in a car warmed him. *Whoever it is, they'll see I'm lost and help. Country folk are friendly.*

Oliver approached the house. It was no manor—just a small cottage with a light bulb shining above the door. A light was shining through a tiny gap in the curtains and a small car was parked by the side of the house. 'A convertible out here? Might as well wear a pair of flip-flops on a hike,' he chuckled.

He walked up the two concrete steps to the front door. He pulled his phone out of his jacket pocket to check the time. *It's late. What if they're asleep?* He rehearsed what to say to whoever would open the door—sure to leave out any talk of hallucinations or the paranormal. He was a Londoner who had gotten lost and needed directions or, preferably.

He decided to try. He knocked three times and slipped his hand back into his pocket's warmth. He waited. *What if they're asleep?* He shook. Was it the cold, or the thought of an old man answering the door with a hunting rifle? *That'd be bad!*

A faint noise made its way through the door. Oliver placed his ear up to wood. *What was that? Was it people talking? Music?* Whatever it was, it was coming from inside. *Perhaps they didn't hear me.* He knocked louder. A minute passed. Then he heard approaching footsteps. Suddenly, the door swung open and light poured out onto the dark porch.

He was blind.

18

OLIVER RUBBED HIS eyes as the light cascaded down upon him. *Please don't be an angry old man with a gun!* He managed to squint out of one eye and saw a thoroughly feminine silhouette dressed in a skirt that ended above the knees and holding, what looked to be, a cigarette.

'Don't just stand there, freezing ya scrawny bum off, get in here!' she scolded and turned back into the house.

Oliver's eyes adjusted to the light as he stepped over the threshold and into the house. He recalled the speech. 'Hello. I apologise for disturbing, but I'm not from around here and I—'

'Leave ya jacket and shoes at the entrance,' her voice interrupted. 'I don't want ya bringin' no mud in.'

'Sorry, I'm lost and need help. If you could just point me—'

'What's it with ya English boys? her raspy but playful voice called from the next room. 'C'mon sweetheart, take your shoes off and get in here.'

Oliver felt little choice in the matter. He removed his shoes, hung his jacket on an empty hook, and walked into a kitchen. It was well lit, warm, and a radio on the counter was filling the room with classic rock.

He looked over at the woman who was rolling out dough on the kitchen island. She was young—perhaps just a few years older than Oliver. She wore a black leather skirt, fashionable shoes, and a frilly top he didn't know the name of. What drew his attention were her shades and cigarette—neither of which seemed to impede her from baking in the least.

Oliver found her attractive—in a dangerous sort of way.

He cleared his throat. 'Hello, my name is Oliver. I don't know if you were expecting someone else, but I'm lost and need some help.'

The woman looked up at him. 'Hello, Oliv-uh!' she said, 'My, you're muddy! Are ya as dirty on the inside as ya are on the out?'

'Huh, dirty? Excuse me, do I know—'

'Water, tea, or cawffee?' she interrupted.

Oliver's head tilted, and his brow furrowed. 'Come again?'

'Wha? Ya don't drink nothin'? It's tea, cawffee, or water?'

Her accent was a peculiar American one. *What is it exactly?*
Chicago? Boston? New Jersey? One of those places on the other side of
the Atlantic where females bleed attitude.

'Ah, I see. Tea, coffee, or water. Well, that's kind of you. But
I was only hoping you could point me on my way.'

'Ya gonna leave me here all by my lonesome? Who's gonna
help me eat these cookies?'

'Oh, well, I'm sure they're quite delicious and—'

'Ya want me to eat them all by myself and get fat?' she asked,
holding her cigarette between her two fingers.

'No, no! I wouldn't want you to get, you know, too big.'

'Good. Then ya can help me eat 'em. Have a seat.'

Though he was still eager to be on his way, a force—perhaps
the woman's intense personality—seemed to push Oliver
towards the kitchen table. The wooden table was simple with a
bit of lace, a tea light, a watch, a driver's license, and a half-full
ashtray. He pulled out a chair and took a seat.

He watched his hostess jotted busily about the kitchen
focused on her baking project. Every so often she'd bend over
and peer into the oven to monitor her creation. Oliver thought
himself lucky to be perfectly seated to enjoy a delightful view of
her legs and leather-skirted backside whenever she did so. The
butterfly tattoo on the back of her calf served as a nice
decoration to her finely sculpted limbs. *Life gives us these gifts*, he

mused. But, more than her fine shape, it was her words that captured Oliver's attention—she talked endlessly to herself while working.

'The oven is makin' this kitchen hot as hell. Yeah know, why do people say that, anyway? Huh? Do they know if hell is hot? What if it's cold enough to freeze ya tits off? Who works there, anyway? Does hell have staff who run the place? I wonder if their workers are organised. Do they have those damned diversity quotas there? Bet they do. That'd be a gas. I can see it now "I'm sorry, but if ya don't have enough transgender, disabled, midget-demons of colour tormenting people, then I'm gonna have to boycott this eternal destiny." Ha! Boycott hell.'

Finally, she opened the oven door, took a tray out and slid the new one in. She stood straight, turned to Oliver, and winked. 'Hope ya enjoyed the show,' she said with a smirk. 'Decide what ya wanna drink yet?'

Oliver ignored her first comment. 'Coffee. Black, please.'

'Black as your soul?'

Oliver's eyebrows lifted. 'Excuse me?'

'I'm only jokin', sweetheart.'

'Oh, yes, of course.'

'Good to see ya ain't racist.'

'Huh?'

'Ya know as in, "I take my coffee like I take my men?" Ya take it black? Jeez, relax. Goodness-sakes. Ya shakin'. English boys are so fragile—ya'd melt at the North Pole.'

'Oh, I see. Sorry. You were joking. Ha, ha, yes,' he said with a laugh that sounded fake even to him. 'With the accent and the shades, it's hard to tell.'

'What accent?' she said with a straight and face.

She carried two mugs over and clapped them on the table. 'Here ya are.' She sat down across from Oliver as he lifted the mug up to his face. The smell, like incense, enveloped him. Oliver smiled and took a sip while looking at her over the rim.

An unexpected but pleasant surprise, he mused.

As he set his mug down, he remembered The Ebony Mane and the filming. 'I appreciate your hospitality. Truly. But I can't stay. I need to be at a manor not far from here.'

She puffed her cigarette and tapped it into the ashtray. 'A manor? Sounds grand. Ya goin' to a party?'

Oliver shook his head. 'No, it's not a party. It's a film project I'm producing.'

'Producing? A film-producer has come to my house? Wozers!'

Oliver couldn't tell if she was teasing him or not. 'Actually, I'm just a film student,' he said, playing ti safe. 'But this project could set me up for a career. That's why it's important I get to that manor soon. A band is waiting for me.'

'Well, isn't this a girl's lucky day? A film producer with his own band? What an exciting life ya must have!'

With his ego freshly stroked, Oliver grinned and shrugged his shoulders bashfully while he floated down Flirting River. 'Well, it's not too glamorous. But I suppose a lot of people would consider me fortunate.'

She smiled back. 'I bet they would.'

Oliver placed his elbows on the table and leaned forward. 'I like your tattoo,' he said with as much swag as he could muster.

'Ah, thanks. It likes ya too,' she said with one of those smiles that all guys hope to receive when they flirt. 'So, will ya wait a minute for my cookies or not?'

Oliver tightened his grip on the mug as his heart rate increased. The band suddenly seemed less urgent. 'Your cookies? Hm. I suppose the others can wait a few minutes. You don't seem like terrible company.'

'Oo, so generous with ya words.'

An idea flashed through Oliver's mind. 'Would you like to come with me? I'm sure the band wouldn't mind. It'd give you a chance to see a real film set,' he said, hoping to impress her.

'Oh, Mr Producer, you tryin' to seduce me or somethin'?'

Seduce? Oliver swallowed the knot in his throat. 'Well, I was just wondering if—'

'I've heard about ya types with your castin' couches for actresses. Am I to be ya next victim? Are ya tyin' to—'

Oliver sat up straight. His sense of caution roared back. 'No! I was just inviting you to see the band. That's all!'

'Oh, I see,' she said cooly as she took a deep puff of her cigarette. 'So, how are ya gonna get us there?'

'Get us there? Oh, well, as I was saying, I got lost walking. I saw your convertible and was hoping you might drive me, or us, over to the house. It's a large manor a mile or two south of here. I was hoping you might know where it is.'

'Yeah, I know the place. The owner's always rentin' it out.'

Oliver's face lit up. 'You know it? That must be it! So, can you drive us over there when we're done with the biscuits?'

'First, they're cookies. What's it with you Brits and ya "biscuits"? Secondly, no. I can't drive ya.'

Oliver deflated like a slashed tire. 'Oh?' He hoped she might explain why, but she just sat there smoking. 'Perhaps I should head off. The coffee's great and the bisc, uh, cookies smell lovely, but people are waiting.'

'I can't take ya to the manor cause my car don't work.'

'Oh?' Oliver asked, curiously. 'How do you get around out here? There's not exactly great bus service.'

'For the time bein', I'm dependin' on a friend for rides to get places. Shall I ring him up? He can getcha a lift to ya manor.'

'Thanks. But I imagine it's too late to ring anyone.'

'Don't worry. My friend, he's a late-night fella. He's got a pickup truck that can fit all three of us. I'm sure he'd love to meet ya—ya bein' a big producer and all,' the woman said, pulling out a phone.

'Well, OK. But only if you're sure he won't mind.

She stabbed a series of digits and held the phone to her ear.

'Hello? Hey boss, it's me. How's ya meetin'?... Yeah, no kiddin'. Well, a guy, Oliv-uh, showed up at the house... He's lost. Says he's a producer. Any chance ya could give us lift to the manor? The one near the highway? ... Great, see ya in a bit. I got some gingerbreads comin' outta the oven... ya also left ya driver's license and watch with me, again!... Yeah, I know... Bye.' She put her phone down. 'Don't worry. He's comin'.'

He was happy to be getting a lift, but not that another guy was in the picture. 'You know my name, but I realise that I've failed to get yours.'

When she said her name, Oliver's heart skipped a beat.

'Ex-excuse me?'

She said it again.

Oliver relaxed his grip on the coffee. 'N-no. Tamar? C-can't be,' he muttered as the room began to spin.

19

IT ALL FLASHED through Oliver's mind. Judah, the manor, the name *Tamar*. He fought for the words to speak. 'So you're g-girl!'

'Well sussed, Mr Obvious. Was it the boobs that gave it away?'

'No, I mean, *the* girl. Judah's daughter-in-law. But, you, you're not dead?'

'Dead? Well, that's kinda complicated.'

Oliver stood up from the table placed his hands on his head. 'It's crazy. I'm dreaming again.'

Tamar shrugged her shoulders and smiled. 'Not every day I have an English boy say I'm a dream.'

'Or brain cancer—you may be a hallucination.'

'Now, ya see, that doesn't sound so nice. Ya should've stopped with dreamin'. Why don't ya sit back down.'

'This isn't real. I need to get out of here!' Oliver stepped towards the hallway.

'Please, have a seat.'

'Listen, I don't know who or what you are. But I have to leave. Now!'

He took his first step towards the hallway when Tamar got out of her seat, grabbed him by his shirt, and slammed her lips onto his. It was a long, heavy kiss. At frist, Oliver was shocked by her action. Then, a sense of warmth filled his body. Finally, a feeling of healthy but controlled excitement began to stir within him.

That's when she pushed him back. 'Now how ya feel?'

Oliver grinned. 'Um, better?'

'Good.'

'Thanks, that *was* great. But, um, I still have questions. I don't understand what's happening and it may be best for my sanity and my schooling if I go.'

She pointed to the chair. 'Have seat, England. I need to talk with ya first.' Oliver looked at the chair and then at the hallway. His mind told him to leave, but the warmth pulsating from his lips stirred a desire to hear what she had to say.

He glanced at the hallway and then sat. 'OK, but only for a little bit.'

'Wonderful choice.'

'Thanks, but I'm still confused. How do I know this is real?'

'Was that kiss not genuine enough for ya?'

Oliver blushed as he cleared his throat. 'Well, I suppose it was. Not hallucination like—and warmer than how I imagined kissing a, well a—'

'A phantom?'

'I don't mean to be disrespectful but, yes, warmer and firmer that how a phantom would kiss—not that I believe in such things,' he was quick to remind himself.

'I'll take it as a compliment,' she said with a nod and a confident smile. 'As for *what* I am, let's just say I'm what I always was only more so. But, as for *who* I am, well, that's part of why I'm here—I need to talk with ya about my life.'

'What's the other reason?'

'We need to talk about your life too.'

'Oh,' Oliver said, looking down. 'That again. Why exactly?'

'Look at ya. Ya miserable. Ya miserable and proud in the way that only smart and creative types can be. Ya wear ya angst on ya sleeve like it's a badge of honour. Ya act like ya soul is too sophisticated or sensitive for this harsh world. Ya unhappy, but ya arrogant about it.'

'Uh, that's quite a-an observation.'

'I got a few more.'

'Can we at least start off talking about you instead of me? Judah said you had... abilities.'

'Abilities? Yeah, I might have a couple. But context is queen.'

'So, you'll tell me your side? Judah told me you married his son for money and that he killed you. Is that right?'

A buzzer rang and Tamar popped up off her chair. 'The last gingerbreads! Want me to bring some over with more cawffee?' she asked, grabbing his mug as she darted to the counter.

'Um, actually, I've had en—,' he began.

'More java comin' up!' she declared and began to pour. 'So, you've decided to stay and listen. But I gotta warn you upfront, my life ain't always been pretty. I may say some things that could upset your delicate sensibilities.'

Oliver rolled his shoulders back and stuck his chin up. 'I think I can handle it,' he said, attempting to lower his voice just a notch. 'I've come across some rough patches myself.'

Tamar grinned. 'Yeah, I bet growing up on the mean streets of East Anglia made a gangsta of ya.'

'How'd you know where—'

'I've got connections.'

'Oh. Of course, you do. Well, yes, I grew up surrounded by cow fields, OK? But I still want to hear your story. And then ... then I'll go to the manor.'

'Ya certain, big boy?'

'Yes.'

Tamar brought the coffee and a plate of hot gingerbread cookies to the table. She looked up at Oliver. 'We grew up in a village in a pine forest in the hills of central Canaan. It was several miles from the closest town and was so crappy that it's an insult to crap everywhere to call it crappy.'

20

PEOPLE GO NOWHERE and do nothing where I come from. A big day for us was going down to Adullam to buy supplies which you could only get in town. Seeing as how we didn't have any money, that wasn't often.

None of my friends ever imagined going anywhere grand like Egypt or Ur. We were the rednecks of Canaan. My pop wasn't a skilled worker and no one in the family could read. And me? I was the only one who survived early childhood. Pop was less than thrilled with only having a daughter around to help him with his work in the fields.

I assumed social forces had predestined me to marry another poor hillbilly in exchange for a couple of goats or a donkey. I imagined we would work the land and try to keep ourselves and our children from starving. But I hated that thought. I dreamt about getting out. Even moving to Adullam would've been an improvement, but I never thought I'd have the chance.

Then I met Er. It was a typical Canaanite party—probably not too different from how young people party in London. I was fifteen and getting near the age when pop would marry me off—so I was trying to enjoy my youth while I still could. I was at the party with some friends, and a group of boys were checking us out. It flattered my friends, but all I saw were losers.

"Hey girl, do you have a raisin? No? How about a date then?"

It was wearisome.

But Er was part of this group. I'd never spoken with him before, but I'd heard about him: that he had his pop's foreign money and his mother's Canaanite morals. Rumours were that he was wild, spoiled, and violent. But, hey, what the hell, right? The party was boring and I figured hooking up with him would be different.

I didn't scrub up too badly when I was fifteen. What's that? You say I still don't? Ah, that's kind. Well, I knew how to get a boy's attention if I wanted it so, when they approached us, I focused on Er. He was seventeen at the time and getting his attention wasn't hard. Men are simple and Er was hyper with a short attention span. Boys like him are easy to play.

I caught his eyes and he returned my flirtatious look.

'Hey, girl, do you have a raisin?'

Really? Is he this stupid? I fought back the sigh, smiled, and batted my eyelashes. 'No, I'm afraid I don't.'

He smiled confidently. 'How about a date then?'

I laughed—on the outside. We had a few drinks together. Maybe it's more accurate to say he drank a lot, and I sat next to him with a cup of beer in my hands. We had only just met, but he put his hands all over me. He was creepy, but his story intrigued me. It turned out his dad was more than just a better-than-average farmer who had moved into the area. His family had real wealth and connections all over the world. His great grandfather had originally come from Ur and had only moved to Canaan after his god—a strange Creator-God—told him to. Can you imagine that? I needed to be sure I heard that right.

'So he left Ur to move out here?' I asked, disbelieving.

'Yeah, ha! Ain't that something. Grandpa Abe got bored with the city and started hearing voices. You want more beer?'

'Nah, I'm good. But, here, ya can have some more.'

'Thanks, you're kinda pretty,' he muttered, already wasted.

'Ah, thanks. You're pretty too. Now, just so I understand, you're the firstborn. And so is your pop, that right?'

I couldn't believe it. This boy was set to inherit wealth. A lot! I'm not sure he was supposed to tell me all that, but boys betray many secrets when they're drunk or horny—and I made sure he was both.

Er fascinated me. Not him so much—but his background. I didn't know anyone with connections like his. As we talked, his hands dancing up and down my body, I wrestled with a choice. Do I splash my beer in his face, call him a pig, and walk off? Or, do I see if I can get this nut-job to marry me?

I wasn't sure I could ever love him. But I didn't wanna merely survive. I wanted to live. That meant leaving—or at least having enough to eat between harvests and having nice clothes.

Would it be worth it? To me, yes. Sure, I suspected he would be the type to hit me when he didn't get what he wanted. Would he become bored with me and sleep with prostitutes? Probably. I knew it might be a loveless marriage. But that wasn't too strange. Most people from my village didn't marry for love—even if we longed for it.

I decided to go for it. Maybe his violence and impulsive nature turned other girls off—and maybe he did have the IQ of a rock. I didn't care. I needed to marry that boy.

So I teased him. I played the game. I put enough of myself out there to make him want me, but not so much that he ever felt he had me. Not all the way. It was easy to pull his strings and drive him wild. I insisted that if he wanted all of me, he'd have to marry me. It took a few months of my best efforts, but it finally paid off.

He brought me to his pop. I knew mine would be no problem. He'd be pleased if he could get more than a few animals for me. But Er suspected his would be more reluctant to give his approval. He was right.

When I met Judah, he looked me up and down. Maybe he wanted to see if my body could bear healthy grandchildren or maybe he was looking at my clothes to gauge my family's financial background. Maybe it was something else.

'Where do you come from?' he asked sternly.

'My family lives in the mountains, a few hours from here.'

'What does your father do?'

'His business is agriculture,' I said, trying to make it sound like he was more than just field worker. Making yourself sound important isn't easy when your family is a bunch of nobodies from nowhere. To my pleasant surprise, it turned out that my pop was cousins with someone in his wife's family—so that helped a bit.

Initially, he told Er he was too young to marry. Judah hadn't married till much later in life. In our culture, girls partied with boys their age, but they married older men who could provide them with a home—while they provide the men with babies. That's how it worked. Er's family was wealthy enough to enable him to marry young, but his father was hesitant. He even told Er to visit prostitutes instead.

But Er was persistent. I'd successfully become his obsession. He kicked and screamed until Judah agreed. My father received five donkeys, a princely price by his standards, and we married.

I did it! I'd married the first-born son of a man set to inherit real wealth. I'd secured my future as a matriarch in a family with connections and means. I'd changed my destiny!

Or so I thought.

I moved in with their family. Er and I had our own tent. I got to know his mother and learned my duties. Er had no sisters, so I was the girl of the family. I collected eggs from chickens and helped manage some goats. I had dinner duties regularly. I didn't mind. Er's family ate much better than my family could ever afford to. They had meat, wines, and cheeses at every meal, not just holidays.

I also got to know Er's two brothers.

Onan was my age. He was more clever than Er, but he was cold towards me. He was cold towards everyone. Er could be violent and mean in sudden, spontaneous ways. But Onan was cruel in a more calculating way. He had the brains and might have been better suited to take over the family business. I think he knew that. I got the sense he felt entitled to the right of firstborn because of his superior intellect.

Onan and I understood each other. Don't misunderstand, I don't mean we liked each other! But we were manipulators, him and I. We knew how to get what we wanted. Not through direct combat like Er, but with calculated words and deeds. The way he looked at me early on told me he knew that I didn't love Er. He knew why I'd married him.

Onan didn't judge me for being a gold-digger. Had he been a woman, he'd have done the same. At dinner times, I'd know when he was manipulating a conversation—and he'd know when I was. We were male/female versions of the other. And therefore natural enemies.

Then there was Shelah. He was wonderful!

'Are you my new sister?' he asked. 'I've never had a sister.'

'Your new sister-in-law, to be precise. How old are you?'

'I'll be fourteen in ten months.'

'Thirteen is a wonderfully awkward year. You're gonna need a big sister to pick on ya, OK squirt?'

'You're nice. And pretty.'

I rubbed his head. 'We're gonna get along just fine.'

I loved him. Shelah was the little brother you could be playful with. With him, I didn't fear the temper I did with Er or the cold calculations I did with Onan. Shelah was open-hearted and caring. He was a younger friend and a fresh breath of innocence in my new life.

But none of this lasted long. Three months after our wedding, Er was dead.

21

I DON'T KNOW how it happened. The evidence pointed to it being a bear. Er was the type who found pleasure in tormenting animals. Perhaps he'd teased a cub. Who knows? He was dead.

Judah lost his mind. Er was his firstborn. Of course, he grieved—the whole family did. But, for Judah, it wasn't just sorrow and loss. He seemed tormented by it—like he was afraid. Er's death had a significance that was hidden from the rest of us.

I was there when the servants who found Er brought Judah his son's clothes. He went hysterical. Afterwards, he looked over his shoulder for days. It was more than sorrow, but what?

Then there was me.

I was just sixteen and already a widow. I mourned my husband. No, that's not true. I pretended to mourn him. It was the expected thing. You might cry out of shock, but it's hard to mourn someone you never loved. If I mourned anything, it was that he died before I was pregnant. I was a widow without a child. My stomach churned with the anxiety of not knowing my future. Would I lose everything I'd fought so hard to get?

Judah and his wife sat me down and gave me a choice. There was a tradition for circumstances like these. It'll sound strange to your ears, but where I came from, it wasn't unusual. You see, children were security. Because of that, a tradition emerged that took care of childless widows. Not all families practised it, but the noble ones did.

The tradition worked like this: if a man died and left a widow behind without children, the man's closest brother would get her pregnant in the name of her deceased husband. That way she could have someone to look after her in old age and the dead brother would have a legal descendant.

The tradition had legal implications. The son to be born would be the legal son of the dead brother—not the biological father. You follow me? I understood this even before Judah and his wife sat me down around the fire in their tent.

'Tamar, we're giving you a choice,' Judah said. 'The first option is that you return to your family. I will send several animals and items of gold back with you to ensure your provision and economic security.'

I nodded. 'Thanks. That's kind. What's the second option?'

'The second is our custom. But I don't expect you to follow it as I know it might be distasteful.'

'I know what it is.'

Judah took a deep breath. 'Perhaps you do. It would mean that you stay with our family and that Onan performs the duty of getting you pregnant on Er's behalf.'

I grimaced at the mention of Onan's name. When I did I thought I saw a glimmer in Judah's eye. Now, looking back, I know I wasn't imagining. Even then, I could detect which option Judah wanted me to choose. He knew my dislike of Onan and was right to assume that the thought of sleeping with him until I got pregnant was a horror. I looked into the fire and weighed up the possibilities.

If I chose the first option, Onan would become the one to inherit from Judah. But, if I chose the second and became pregnant with a son, then my son, not Onan, would take over.

Onan was smart and I sensed that Judah wanted to hand everything over to him. He saw me as a gold-digger and I suppose he wasn't wrong. But I sensed it was more than just that. It was almost like something about me frightened him.

Either way, the choice was mine. I could take the money and return to my village—or stay, have sex with Onan, and fight for my place as the next matriarch.

I looked back up at Judah and his wife. 'This is difficult. Will you allow me one day to consider?'

Judah pressed his lips together. He'd hoped I'd choose the first option and leave straight away. He said, 'Very well. It's a big choice. Let me know by tomorrow evening.'

Then he and his wife got up from the fire and left.

I didn't sleep much that night. Going back to my tiny village in the pine forest felt like giving up. But why? If I went back with wealth, wouldn't that satisfy me? Plus, what if it took me a long time to get pregnant? Did I wanna be knocking boots with Onan for a year or two? Course not! The thought of giving my body over to his reptilian hands gave me nightmares.

By morning, I'd made my decision. I'd take the first option and leave with the wealth. I decided that I wouldn't wait until evening—I'd tell Judah after breakfast.

I went to the communal table to get some food. It was then that I saw Shelah. *Now there's the one person I'll miss!* He was standing near the table with one of his uncles as a few of Judah's brothers had come down to Adullam for Er's funeral. Normally, meeting their extended family would've fascinated me. But, given that I had been playing the role of the bereaved widow, I hadn't had the chance to talk with them.

I came up behind Shelah and hugged him.

He smiled. 'Good morning, Tamar!'

'Hey shorty,' I said, giving him a wink.

'Have you met my uncle Benji yet?'

I turned and gave a small bow towards his uncle. He was a lot younger than Judah. 'I met ya briefly last week, but we haven't spoken much yet,' I said.

Benjamin returned the bow and looked at me with a kind sincerity. 'I'm sorry for your loss. It must be difficult to lose someone you love and face widowhood at such a young age.'

His genuine care surprised me. 'Thanks for coming down for my husband's funeral.'

'It's the least we could do,' Benjamin replied. 'We only wish we knew you better. We all miss Judah and would love for him to move home—with all of you, of course.'

Benjamin's words grabbed my interest. 'May I join ya two for breakfast? I wanna hear more about the family.'

'It would be an honour,' Benjamin said.

I sat with Shelah and Benjamin as he told me about Abraham, Isaac, and Jacob. He told me how his father wrestled with an angel, how Judah's sister Dinah was raped, and how wild animals had killed his full-blooded brother, Joseph, when he was small—a strange coincidence in light of how Er died.

Benjamin also talked about the God their family worshipped—something Judah never did. The God he spoke of sounded nothing like the gods of the Canaanites. I was fascinated. I'd only ever heard of Him the first night I met Er and he told me why his great-grandfather Abraham had left Ur. It seemed like we talked all morning. Benjamin was kind and patient to answer all my questions.

They got up and left. I stayed seated and thought about what I'd heard. Somehow, just listening to that story, changed something in me. It was a story I wanted to be a part of.

I went to Judah. 'I've made my decision,' I said, interrupting his conversation with a servant.

'Excuse me, just a moment' he said to them and then turned to me. 'I didn't expect to hear from you until tonight.'

'I've decided, and I'm sure of my choice.' I replied.

'Very well. What have you chosen?'

'I wanna be a part of your family.'

He looked puzzled. 'But why? I told you I'd send animals and gold to you and your family. You'd lack nothing. I know you and Onan aren't exactly—'

'I'll have to deal with Onan. It's not just about money. I wannna be a part of your family. Ya have something my family doesn't—even if it's something you never talk about.'

Judah's brow furrowed. 'I don't understand what you mean,' he grumbled back, 'But it is your choice. I'll respect it.' He turned and scuttled off, kicking dirt as he went.

I skipped back to my tent. My heart raced with excitement over the decision I'd made. Somehow this family was special in a way that mine wasn't—and it wasn't just the money.

Little did I know that things were about to get much darker than I could ever imagine.

22

I KNEW IT would be unpleasant. Sex with Onan, that is. But I didn't know how unpleasant. Judah called us both into his tent. What gave me the courage to face it was knowing that I'd chosen this and, that if I bore a son, glory awaited me.

'Onan, do you understand what's required of you? You must perpetuate the name and line of your brother, Er.'

'Yes, father,' he said with a nod.

Then Judah looked at me. 'Tamar, you know what you've chosen. You will be with Onan until you become pregnant.'

'I understand,' I said.

'Whose tent will you sleep in?'

'Can it be my tent?' I asked, hoping that the familiarity of the surroundings would make it more bearable.

'Do you have any objections, Onan?' Judah asked.

'No, sir,' Onan replied.

'So it shall be.'

'Thank you, father,' Onan replied and then, I swear, the perv winked at me—and then skittered out of the tent.

*****

That night, he showed up at my tent door. 'May I enter?'

'Yes, come in,' I replied, trying to be optimistic that it might not be as bad as I'd feared. I'd been unsure how to prepare the tent. Should I have made it warm and cosy? Or should I have made things clinical and professional? I opted for something between the two.

He stepped into the tent and, for a moment, we stared into each other's eyes. He had a blank expression on his face. *Maybe, since we're doing this for Er, we can put past hostilities behind us. Maybe he'll be tender given the circumstances.*

But then he smiled. And it wasn't the friendly, warm type of smile meant to reassure me. It was the smile an alligator has when it sees its prey. He didn't wanna comfort me. He wanted me to be afraid.

'Strip!' he commanded.

May heart sank and I froze. *So this is how it's gonna be?* I considered running from my tent. But to what end? Wasn't my goal to get pregnant?

'Take. Your. Clothes. Off. Now,' he uttered slowly. I obeyed him. How could I not? This is why he'd come.

I undressed and stood before him naked. Everything in me wanted to cover myself from his stare, but I mustered my courage. I wasn't going to let him see me quake. *You've chosen this!* I kept repeating to myself. My hair hung down over my breasts. It was the only hint of modest protection I allowed myself in that moment.

His clothes were still on. He reached out, pushed my hair aside, and grabbed me. The coldness of his hand sent shivers through my body—and not the good kind. 'Nice,' he smiled.

Suddenly, he smacked me hard across the face and pushed me back onto the pillows on my floor. He undressed as I laid looking up at him. 'You will not find this fun. You will not enjoy this. This will hurt you,' he said with no emotion before descending on me.

I won't go into unnecessary details. It was bad. I was used to aggressive sex. Er had been a wild guy and, since I knew he liked me, I didn't mind too much. At times, I even enjoyed it.

But this was different. There was no warmth. No affection. No sense that what he was doing anything noble on behalf of his brother. He smacked me, hurt me, and unleased all his lust inside my tent.

The process was as painful as it was long. He took his time. I made my body limp and refused all tears. But, when it got to the end—when it got the point where I could tell he was about to climax—he withdrew from me, pushed me forward, and unloaded himself on the floor of my tent.

What had just happened? my mind screamed in confusion. He was on his knees, panting. We looked at each other and I held his gaze. His eyes cut into me like ice daggers, but I refused to turn away.

'Se-see you to-omorrow,' he said, still catching his breath. He dressed and left my tent with me on the floor.

I lay there, naked, bruised, and bleeding. I passed in and out of a dim and dreary sleep that night.

What have I agreed to?

The next night he returned. He didn't ask if he could enter this time. He walked in and, without saying a word, took off my clothes and pushed me down. I wanted to rip his ballsack off, the perv! But how would that help me get pregnant?

Like the first night, he unloaded on the floor.

And that's what terrified me. I'd never encountered darkness like this. I saw he had no intention of getting me pregnant. He wanted to inherit the family leadership, and was refusing to get me pregnant so that his brother wouldn't have a legal heir!

He didn't mind using me for sex and humiliating me. I don't know if it was about power or pleasure or both. But he had no intention of making a child and I wondered how long this could go on for. I laid there, cold and bruised, night after night, imagining a future where Onan was married with children, leading the family after Judah's death, and where I was nothing more than his forever, childless whore.

I wanted to die. I contemplated suicide. Perhaps that was Onan's hope: to drive me to insanity or death. He was both clever and wicked enough to do such a thing.

I considered murdering him. I fondled a knife one afternoon and hid it under my pillow. But I didn't go through with it. I knew Judah would have an especially cruel form of execution prepared for me if I killed his son.

Night after night I was left in a pool of pain. I questioned why I'd chosen this path. *Why didn't I take the money and return to my family? What had it been about uncle Benjamin's words that had convinced me that this was the better option?*

I'd thought this was a special family, but I saw only darkness. I lost my appetite and spent my days doing chores in a daze.

Shelah noticed. 'Are you OK? You've got a bruise your face.'

'One of the goats kicked me while I was milking it.'

'I'm sorry. You seem tired.'

'I haven't slept well.'

'Is there anything I can do to help?'

Kill your big brother? 'No thanks, shorty. I'll manage.'

It was the worst time of my life. But it lasted less than two months. Then, tragedy struck again—Onan died!

His death was a horror to everyone—to everyone but me, that is. He passed in his sleep with no signs of sickness. I wasn't sad it happened, but it was mysterious.

That's when Judah really lost it—much more than before. At first, I didn't blame him. He'd lost two sons in three months. But his grief differed from his wife's. When Er died, I thought I'd detected fear in him. But now that fear was obvious—as if a spectre was haunted him.

A month after Onan's funeral, Judah called me into his tent. His hands were fidgety and he didn't look me in the eyes. I'd never seen him this way.

'I'll send you back with more donkeys, sheep, and cattle than your family could ever hope for. Your father will be the richest man in his village,' he said, with desperation in his voice.

I bowed before my father-in-law. 'That's kind of ya. But my mind hasn't changed. I still wanna be a part of this family.'

'Shelah? You want Shelah to father your children?' he protested. I winced at the thought. Shelah had only just turned fourteen. He was my little brother. Sleeping together would change all that.

'Yes, he's young. But I've chosen and it's my right to stay.'

Judah didn't contest that. 'Name your price. I'll give you anything to return to your family.' He still avoided my eyes.

'Why are ya eager for me to leave? How have I offended ya?'

'Offended? No. You haven't offended me.'

'Then what is it?'

'My reasons are my own.'

'I don't mean to displease ya, but my destiny is here.'

My words caused Judah to tremble. 'Don't say that!'

'Why?' I yelled, losing control. 'You stupid man! What have I done? I've obeyed the rules of your house and respected your foreign ways. Ya have no right to treat me like this!'

Judah bit his fist and looked to the ground as a long moment passed. Finally, he looked up at me and took a deep breath. 'Let's make a deal.'

'A deal?'

'Shelah is still young. He's a virgin. He's never been out partying with local girls or seen a prostitute. He doesn't know how to be with a woman.' I didn't object. Shelah's inexperience with women contributed to his innocence and was part of why I adored him. I looked to the ground. Judah wanted what was best for Shelah. 'I know,' was all I could muster in reply.

'Then, if you know, do this. Return to your family for a season. You wouldn't want him to lose his innocence or have harm come to him? If you do, I'll call you back once he's ready.

Then you can rejoin our family and become pregnant by Shelah. I'll even send a cow and two sheep home with you to ensure that you're no burden on your father's finances while you're there. That's not so bad, is it?'

I hesitated. I wanted to be a part of this family, but he made sense. I didn't look forward to making a lover of Shelah, but perhaps it would be more bearable once his voice finished changing. A cow and two sheep would also be a big help to my old family. *Judah is just trying to look out for his son, right?*

I bowed. 'I accept your proposal. I'll return home.'

Judah sighed, 'Thank you, Tamar.' And he dismissed me.

As I journeyed back home, my mind replayed the conversation. There was one thing I wish I'd questioned Judah about. It was a question I couldn't quite get out of mind.

What did he mean by saying he didn't want any harm to come to Shelah?

23

OLIVER'S MOUTH HUNG wide. A pile of gingerbread crumbs lay on the table beneath his chin. 'He sent you away? I'm confused. Back at the manor, he told me he'd tried to murder you. Which is it?'

Tamar took a long drag on her cigarette and jabbed it down onto the ashtray where it lay twisted and smoking before reaching for her coffee. 'Patience. There's more to it than that. Judah kept his hands clean from blood ever since that incident with Joseph and he wasn't in any rush to get them dirty again. We haven't gotten to that bit yet. Ya want more cawffee?'

Oliver pushed his mug across the table. 'Yes, please.'

Tamar took both mugs, walked over to the counter, and filled them again from the pot on the burner. 'Things got worse—for everyone involved,' she said over her shoulder. She grabbed a couple more gingerbreads from the tray and returned to the table. 'Here's your cawffee.'

'Thanks.'

'Ya welcome, sweetheart.'

Oliver hugged the hot mug with his fingers and lifted the freshly poured java to his lips and took a delicate sip. 'Perfect.'

Tamar took a bite of her cookie, chewed, and then began to speak with her mouth still half-full of gingerbread. 'So, I've been tellin' ya all about my troubles with men. Hows about ya tellin' me about your issues with Elise?'

'Wait, what?'

'Ya know, your lady friend? The blonde Czech doll who gave ya a lift out here? Where ya taking this relationship?'

'How do you know about, um, never mind. Dumb question. Let me guess, you know everything about me?'

'Not everythin'. Only the top boss knows everthin'. But I know enough to be curious.'

'Well, what do you want to know about her?'

'Like I said, where ya takin' this relationship?'

'Taking it? I'm not taking it anywhere. We're friends.'

'Only, ya not. Ya constantly eye her up and down. Hey, I don't blame ya—she's lovely. But she has feelings for ya too.'

'Friendships between men and women can sometimes have mixed emotions. It doesn't mean I need to formally ask her out.'

'Friendship's great and all, but neither of ya is datin' anyone else, and neither of ya is married. What gives? There's somethin' other than just friendship goin' on, ain't there?'

'Maybe. I don't know. It just hasn't happened yet.'

'It hasn't happened yet because ya keep treatin' her like she's ya mom and ya lack the nuts to take responsibility.'

Oliver tensed up as if he was back in primary school and sitting in the headmaster's office. 'No, not like my mum.'

'Well, not exactly. But ya know what I mean. Ya get her to drive ya around everywhere. She helps ya with school projects and buys ya cawffee whenever the two of ya go out.'

'Her job pays better than mine!'

'She has a job is what ya mean! Ya've been unemployed four months now.'

'School has kept me busy!'

'Yeah, yeah, yeah. You're a wuss, Oliv-uh. And ya messin' up this girl because of it.'

'I'm not hurting her! She enjoys our friendship.'

'Ya inspired her with last year's project. She thought maybe ya was different, that ya had some depth to ya. But she's just been hangin' round ya hopin' that you're gonna man up and ask her out the right way. But ya never do. Ya want the affection of a woman without having to take responsibility for a relationship. What's the longest ya've ever had a genuine relationship for? Three months when ya was seventeen? Jeez! I've had headaches that have lasted longer.'

'I'm only a student, I'm twenty! You want me to get married or something? I'm not ready for that.'

'That's because ya effeminate, Oliv-uh.'

Oliver winced at the term. 'Did you say "effeminate"?'

'Yep.'

'OK. What exactly do you mean by that?'

'Ya unwillin' to put aside pleasure to do what's right. Elise likes ya, but she's losing respect for ya—fast! And a girl like her needs a fella of character she can look up to. Sure, some gals see a guy who's angry or rebellious and think it's strength. Other women get pleasure out of controlling a weak guy they'll never respect. Elise ain't like that. She's from an old-fashioned home and wants a man of conviction she can admire. She thought, after reading what ya wrote last year, that ya might be a fella like that. But you're slowly breakin' her heart.'

'How do you know?'

Then Tamar did the most unexpected of things. She lit a new cigarette, took a deep drag, leaned across the table, and blew the smoke right into Oliver's face.

24

OLIVER SHUTTERED BACK in his chair, coughing. His eyes burned with smoke as he rubbed them furiously.

As he slowly reopened them, he saw a cloud of smoke hovering over the table like a dense fog over a country field. In the middle of the cloud was, what seemed to be, something like a window into a sitting room. The room was warmly decorated for the holiday season and, in the centre of the room, sat two women: a younger woman and a middle-aged woman. He instantly recognized Elise as the younger woman. Her head was leaned back against the older woman who had her arm around her.

'What's this?' Oliver asked amazed.

'Ya seein' into Elise's home.'

'She's sad. I can see their lips moving like their talking, but I can't hear their conversation.'

'They're havin' a late-night girly sesh. Her mom is advisin' her to move on with her life and give her attention to someone other than you—and she's considerin' it.'

Tamar's words fell on him like a bucket of bricks. The thought of Elise being with another guy cut his breath short. 'But, why would she do that? Elise and I have fun together.'

'She's lookin' out for her daughter. There's nothin' wrong with pleasure. But ya addicted to it. She's hurtin' because ya refuse to grow up.'

Oliver stared at Elise's moving lips as a tear came down her cheek. He closed his eyes and turned his head away. 'No, please, don't show me this. I didn't mean to hurt her. I thought she liked my company. Why are you showing me this?'

'I'm here to help—if you'll allow yourself to be helped.'

Oliver rubbed his eyes again and, when he reopened them, the cloud was gone.

'I know about men, Oliv-uh. I know the good and the bad they can do to women. Onan wanted the pleasure and power he felt bein' with me—but without a baby.'

'Wait,' Oliver objected. 'Did you just compare me to the guy who raped you?'

'Was it rape? Maybe. I did consent to the process. But the way he did it was abusive.'

'I'm not abusing Elise!' he retorted.

'Not sexually. Not physically. But emotionally? Relationally? Ya take but don't give.'

Oliver's body tensed. His mind raced to find an excuse he could hide behind to keep Tamar's words from being true. He opened his mouth, but couldn't find the defence he wished he had.

She continued. 'Ya enjoy the sex that comes from porn and hook-ups that comes through parties and dating apps—'

'So what if I do?' Oliver interrupted in a flash of defensiveness. 'I bet you have the same ideas about sex my grandpa does. Don't get me wrong, I love him. But it's a bit too old fashion for today's world. I think people should be free to sleep with whomever they want.'

'Yeah? How's that philosophy workin' out for ya?'

Her question caught him off guard. 'Well, um, I suppose—'

'Ya take pleasure from women, but ya don't protect them. Not emotionally. No, you're not cruel like Onan. You don't take pleasure in causin' pain—ya have a sweet side. But ya hurt people through negligence.'

Oliver remembered how he had manipulated Elise into giving him a lift—with the stolen equipment—out to the manor. His defences cracked. He couldn't hide from the pain he had seen in Elise's face. He reached down into his soul and grasped a white flag. 'OK—you got me on this one.'

'How, exactly?'

'Well, I have been a bit negligent and I need to do better with Elise,' he conceded.

'I'm glad ya can at least admit that much. It's a start, but when a man is effeminate, it affects more than how he treats women. It's his entire life.'

'Really?' Oliver asked, uncertain. 'I mean, I want to be a good man for Elise—I don't want to hurt her anymore. But I don't see how this affects more than her.'

'Why'd ya wait until the last minute?'

'Huh?'

'The project is due next week, and ya're only filming now. If winnin' means so much to ya, why?'

The urge to defend himself erupted within. 'Because I struggle with time management—is that really a moral failing?'

'Ya "struggle with time management"? Is that how ya say that ya're lazy and easily distracted?'

Oliver felt tricked. He'd hoped that by being partially vulnerable, Tamar would ignore his other faults. His jaw tensed and he tried to hold back the profanities. 'I'm not taking character insults from a gold-digger, OK?'

'Calm down, sweetheart. I'm not sayin' this to insult ya. I wanna help. You want people to respect ya as a man, but your life is undisciplined and lazy. Effeminate.'

'Stop pretending you understand!' Oliver barked. 'You're just a strange girl I met tonight. You're probably not even that—you're some nightmare or sickness.'

'Well don't ya say the sweetest things?' she said, sarcasm dripping. 'Even if I'm a mental illness or a dream, I'm still part of ya. If I'm a ghost, or somethin' akin to it, how do ya know what wisdom I might have access to?'

Oliver took a deep breath. He'd been so focused on what she was saying he'd forgotten he wasn't speaking to just any pretty girl. 'OK, you *may* know something about me,' he yielded.

'Thanks. Now, if you'll put ya pride aside, don't ya recognise at least some of what I'm sayin' is true?'

Oliver pressed his lips together and paused before responding. 'You're not wrong. At least, not totally. Yes, I can be undisciplined. Sometimes very much so,' he confessed.

Tamar tilted her head in empathy. 'Now we're makin' progress. Not excusing faults is a manly thing to do.'

Her words encouraged him. 'Thank you.'

'Ya welcome,' she responded with a warm smile.

'May I ask, why are you so interested in my character?'

'The character of humanity is the interest of the Universe.'

Oliver's lips pressed together in cynical disbelief. 'The interest of the Universe? What, are you supposed to an alien now? I'm sure if there's any life out there in deep space, that they have far more interesting things on their mind than how I treat other humans.'

'A man either renouncing or succumbing to effeminacy attracts interest from powers ya now know nothin' about.'

'There's that word again. I'd assumed "effeminate" was a chauvinist insult—like being a woman is something bad. Now you're telling me it's a thing that attracts the attention of extra-terrestrials?'

Tamar smiled. 'Not the E.T. phone type, if that's what ya have in mind. Look, Oli-vuh, I love bein' a woman. Bein' a woman is great—if ya're a woman. But I didn't say "feminine". I said "effeminate"—that's when a man isn't bein' masculine.'

'Masculine? There's another word that has no meaning.'

'It has no meanin' for you—and it shows.'

'It's only culturally constructed concept.'

'Ya learn that on social media? Look, your world is haunted by the idea of masculinity. It's a subject filled with ghostly ideas that the *intoleristas* of your day would like to exorcise. But masculinity and femininity are as much a part of this Universe as light or gravity. Ya can make up all sorts of snazzy slogans and ideologies to try and explain them away, but they're still there and, deep down, ya know it. Look, Oliv-uh, I simply want ya to a man worthy of respect. That's why I'm so blunt with ya.'

Oliver nodded his head. He knew she wasn't speaking nonsense and some of her words sounded like something his grandpa might say. 'OK, I hear you. Go ahead, in what other way do you think I effeminate?'

'Ya fear hard work and failure. Ya don't just fear them, ya run from them. Let's go back: why is it ya only now filming?'

Oliver looked down. 'I thought you said it was because I was lazy.'

'And I think ya agree that's at least partially true, yeah? But there's more. You're afraid to face the possibility that last year's victory was a fluke. Ya afraid ya could never do such a good job again. Ya laziness combined with your fear of failure means ya stay a boy. Bein' a man means ya embrace the risk of failure. As it is, ya avoid risk and try to get by on charm.'

Her accusation was a smack across the face. Oliver was unsure of how to respond. He imagined standing, getting his jacket, and walking out of the house—or at least arguing back.

But he did neither. He looked up, shoulders still heavy, and spoke right into her shades. 'Everything you've said is true. I've been reckless with Elise's emotions, I've avoided hard work like it was a virus, and I don't try hard things because I'm afraid I'll fail. I'm in my twenties now, but I'm nowhere close to being a man. I have no excuse.'

Then Tamar did something he did not expect. She took her shades off and stared straight into his eyes. She had the most beautiful and lively mahogany eyes he'd ever seen. A tear came slowly down her cheek. She reached over and took his hand. A sense of beauty and vulnerability overtook him. That silent minute, staring into her teary eyes, was the most intimate moment he'd ever shared with a woman.

'Oliv-uh, that was the manliest thing I've heard anyone say in a long time,' she finally said and walked to his side of the table. She rubbed his hair back with her hand and placed a kiss atop his forehead. The warmth of it calmed his fears.

She stepped away and his hair tumbled back across his brow. 'Now, perhaps I should finish telling ya about the murder. Ya OK with that?'

'Murder?' Oliver exclaimed, having momentarily forgotten. 'Oh, yes, of course. And also, what did your father-in-law mean when he said he didn't want harm to come to Shelah?'

A deep and familiar voice vibrated through the room. 'Maybe I should explain that myself, Mr Anderson.'

Oliver turned to the hallway.

It was Judah.

25

WITHOUT SO MUCH as a by your leave, Judah walked over and plunked himself behind the table. Oliver flinched.

'Hello, Mr Anderson.'

Oliver felt exposed, having had such an intimate moment with Tamar. 'You again! Are you *trying* to freak me out?'

'Is that what I'm doing?'

'Rather successfully.'

'It's not my main objective, but your squirming is a bonus.'

'You're a freak. Why'd you treat this girl the way—'

Tamar cut in. 'Want something to drink, sweetheart?'

'The usual.'

'Bourbon,' Tamar remarked with a smile. She sauntered over to the cupboards. 'By the way, ya driver's license is on the table.'

'Thanks.'

'Ya better lookin' than ya picture, ya know,' she said with a smile as she grabbed a bottle of Kentucky's finest.

'Thanks. You're better looking than my picture too,' Judah replied. He turned to Oliver. 'You find the coffee here better than at the manor?'

'Of-of course,' Oliver stuttered, still recovering from Judah's surprise entry.

Tamar returned with Judah's drink and plopped it on the table. 'Here ya go. Now don't just sit there, finish the story!'

Oliver cut in. 'Wait, just so I understand, this was your friend?'

'Ya expectin' the Easter Bunny?'

'No, it's just ... guess I should've known.'

'Shall I proceed, Mr Anderson?' Judah inquired.

Oliver sighed. 'This better be good,' he said with his arms crossed. 'Given all Tamar's told me, you've explaining to do.'

**

I bribed and banished Tamar back to her home village to save my son's life. When Er died, my heart broke and I could no longer suppress the memories of what I'd done to father. He'd loved his son, Joseph, just as I'd loved Er—and now they were both gone. I feared Heaven's justice and blamed myself for Er's death. Father had told me that the God he worshipped was one of justice, but the thought that he might actively be working to bring that justice upon me was unbearable.

Then Onan died. Losing him unleashed a terror within. You understand why? Joseph's ghost had found me. He was out to destroy everything I held dear. Nothing was safe! He'd take everything I held dear—just as I'd done to father.

How did Joseph's spirit find me, though? Why, after almost twenty years, did he suddenly show up? What was his inroad into our family through which he could bring about such devastation? There was one, simple answer: Tamar.

I'd put the sins of my youth behind me. Joseph's cries were a distant memory. Then Tamar came, and I lost Er to wild animals—just as I'd told father about Joseph. Then I gave her to Onan, and I lost him. She was the common denominator. She was the one channelling Joseph's ghost to torment our family and bring it to nothing. So I sent Tamar away—scared of the curse she carried. But a man who runs from his fears often finds he's only taken a short-cut to them.

Several months went by and it seemed like the storm had passed. My wife and I had finished grieving our oldest two sons and focused on Shelah. I dared to hope good days were ahead. Our plans were clear: Shelah would marry well and my wife and I would enjoy our grandchildren. We dared to hope.

But then it came and, oh God, did it ever come! My wife got ill. At first, I didn't think much of it; she'd been sick before and always recovered. But, this time, she wasn't getting better. I sent for doctors as far away as Egypt. But to no avail. She took all sorts of medicine, but her health continued to decline.

I lost sleep. I designated the running of the family business to my servants. I sat by my wife's side and cared for her. Was Tamar working her dark magic from her family village? Was the curse of Joseph permanently on me? Would I never be able to pay for my sins?

My wife never got better. After a year of fighting, she died.

I mourned her. We didn't have the best of marriages. I'd found her attractive in her youth, but I wasn't always in love with her the way my father had been with Rachel. But the marriage worked. We raised sons and got along most of the time. Our final year, when I nursed her, was our closest.

I mourned losing her but, more than that, I despaired what the curse my sins had made. I'd dug a pit to hell and now I was falling in it.

I wondered if this curse would be with me forever. I'd lost two sons and my wife in just a couple of years. It seemed unfair! I'd only taken one son from my father. So why was I losing everything? Would Joseph be satisfied with my wife's death?

Two months after the funeral, a couple of events happened that comforted me. First, a wealthy father approached me about his daughter marrying Shelah. My son was now close to seventeen and, though that was still a young age, it wasn't too early to begin discussions—I think, deep down, I was hoping grandchildren would reinvigorate me.

My second source of comfort was my old friend, Hirah. He visited me and made me laugh in a way that I hadn't in a long time. He invited me up to a sheep-shearing festival at Timnah. Now, for a city boy like you, it may be difficult to appreciate what that means. But the week of sheep shearing is a big party for country lads. It takes place in the Spring when the sheep no longer need their wool, and shepherds bring their flocks together to shear and sell it.

I accepted his invitation and headed for the hills. I loaded my donkey with some of our best skins of wine and choice cuts of meat and off I went. It was a fantastic week with the lads—I saw old friends I hadn't seen in years. We drank, ate, drank, told stories, and drank. It was the type of week that makes an older-middle aged man feel young again. My problems dissolved in their company. I laughed in a way that I hadn't since Er died.

There was one embarrassment to the whole week—an unfortunate incident. On the first day, on my way up to the mountains, I passed a tent set up near a river. I recognised the sort of tent it was. It was ornate with a cloud of incense creeping about it. It was a whore's tent and I smiled at the sight of it.

Then a girl came out. And, wow! Her looks went through me like a knife. A veil circled about her face revealing only her eyes. But what eyes! They were dark, painted, and gloriously enchanting. She danced in front of me, showing off her legs, arms, and neck. Her movements intoxicated me. She came close and flaunted every uncovered inch of her body.

I'd been faithful to my wife while she was alive. But now a young woman—young, judging from her lithe body—was inviting me to herself. Sexual energy pulsated through me like I hadn't felt in years—and a forgotten madness filled me again.

'Let me sleep with you!' The words stumbled out of my mouth.

'How much am I worth to you?'

'It's, um, sheep-shearing season,' I blubbered out. 'I-I can send you a sheep from my flock once I arrive at Timnah.' Desire had taken over my reason. A whole sheep is an unheard-of price for an hour with a whore. Typically, a loaf of bread will do.

She nodded. 'What will you give me as security until I get it?'

I looked about me. What could I give her? Had I been sane, I'd have offered her a skin of wine. But her allure had scrambled my reason. 'Whaddya want?' I muttered—a calf to the slaughter.

'How about your ring and cord?'

'My ring and cord?' Even in my sexual frenzy, it seemed a big ask. These were personal items, like a man's ID.

'Yes, your ring and cord—then I'll be sure to get my sheep.'

The way she talked, it seemed to make sense. 'OK,' I uttered and handed the items to her. I would've given her my blood just as long as I could've gotten naked with her in that tent.

The sex—what can I say?—it transported me to the realms of bliss. I hadn't been with a young woman since, well, my wife was young. Her firm body and intense energy rocketed me into long-forgotten heights of sexual bliss. I left the tent feeling like a new man. *And this is just the beginning of party week!*

But the next day I encountered a problem. I sent a friend down to Enaim with the promised sheep, but the girl was gone. We searched for her. Those items I'd given as a deposit were important but, search as we may, we couldn't find her.

The local folks began to laugh at us. 'What sort of fool leaves his ring and cord with a prostitute?'

Me, it would seem. I'd come up to this week to laugh, not to be laughed at—so I dropped the whole issue.

Other than that mistake, the week was great. The friends, the banter—it was good for my soul. I returned home with a fresh determination to go forward in life and plans for Shelah marrying. Our business was doing well. Surely I'd already atoned for my sins. Now I could move on.

The following weeks and months were happy ones. A couple of good business contracts came my way and I was able to trade my sheep for an impressive load of grain. Shelah was now a young man and I connected with him deeper than ever. We'd stay up late, talking by the fire, and together we put our losses behind us and thought of the future.

I spoke with the father that had approached me concerning the marriage of our children and plans began to go forward slowly. Nobody was in a rush. Shelah was seventeen and the girl was fourteen. The wedding was still a year away, but we all wanted to make it huge.

That summer, Shelah was the one by my side as we sought fresh pasture for our livestock. I was proud to see him commanding the servants and take responsibility for the business he'd one day inherit. Not only was he competent with the animals, but Shelah was good with people—better than I ever was. Local leaders liked him and I imagined the family growing in power under his leadership. In five years, Shelah would take over, and I could pass into semi-retirement. A bright vision of the future enthralled me and our household had joy once again.

It was only a matter of weeks until that life came crashing down.

26

THE GIRL'S FATHER appeared unexpectedly. When I saw him in the distance, I smiled and assumed he was visiting to drink and dream with me about the wedding of our children. But, when he got closer, I knew something was wrong. He got off his camel and approached me with eight of his servants. His face grimaced and he spat on the ground before shouting, 'Judah! What is this you've done?'

I was taken aback. The man had only ever spoken to me with the deepest respect.

'I don't know what you are talking about, friend. What grievance can there be between you and me?'

'What grievance? I've heard Shelah has an outstanding obligation to impregnate the widow of his deceased brother. If this is true, it changes our plans! It would risk the inheritance rights of any children my daughter would bear.'

He was right. I'd long since chosen to forget Tamar's claim on Shelah. My hand began to twitch. 'W-wait!' I shouted— unsure of what to say. I smiled but was hysterical on the inside. 'Don't worry. The girl won't lay claim to him. I've paid the family well enough.'

'Oh? Is this true? I'm afraid I'll need proof that this widow no longer has any claim before the wedding plans can proceed.'

'As I said, I paid her family well and sent her away.'

'Has she renounced the claim on Shelah before witnesses?'

Both hands were now twitching. 'Not formally,' I replied, in my fight to save Shelah's wedding. 'But I'm certain it's settled.'

He spat on the ground again. 'Either she has legally renounced her claim or she hasn't. I've engaged my daughter to your son under the presumption that Shelah will inherit from you and that my daughter will be his principal wife. If Shelah still has a legal obligation to this girl, then the wedding is off. I won't accept a payoff if there's no public renunciation.'

I attempted a charming smile. 'It's only a technicality. I'll have the widow's legal renunciation before the month's end.'

He stared me, a most unhappy man. 'You'd better!' And, with that, he remounted his camels and hurried off.

I was furious with myself. How could I have overlooked this? I was so optimistic about the future that I'd neglected to clean up the past. I'd pushed it away from my thoughts. I'd wanted

Tamar to accept her life back with her old family so badly that I'd pretended it'd already happened.

Now, the reality was slapping me back in the face.

I took a deep breath and called for my chief servant—an excellent diplomat. I needed to get this fixed, quick, for Shelah's sake. This was an unfortunate setback, but we could still fix it. When he came into my tent, I explained the situation.

'I want you to take two cows and ten sheep to her family.'

'So many?' he asked in unbelief.

'Yes, and after you've delivered them, ask her and her father if she'll make a renunciation before witnesses. Surely her heart is now with her family.'

'I'll do all that you ask, my lord,' he said with a bow and left.

I felt a fool, but I had hope. Two cows and ten sheep were a huge sum. Yes, this was an obstacle to Shelah's future—but it was one I believed we could remove with wealth.

When my servant returned two days later, disappointment weighed heavy on his face.

'What happened?' I demanded.

'I'm sorry, my lord. I gave the gifts as you instructed. The girl's father grinned like a camel in heat. He accepted the gifts you'd sent and said he'd ask his daughter who has her own small house behind theirs—a tiny hut.'

'Yes, and?'

'Well, my lord, he left to speak with her and returned most unhappy. His daughter had refused and he couldn't change her mind. I asked if I could speak with her, I thought that, perhaps, I could persuade her. He returned a few minutes after and told me she refused to see me and that she was demanding her right as a widow from your son Shelah. Her father's face was red, and he struggled to look me in the eye. His inability to reason with his daughter embarrassed him.

'I spoke with him some more, but the girl refused to see me. The father is sympathetic but, according to him at least, she seems determined to have your son. Not being able to address the girl directly, I finished speaking with her father and left.'

My heart pounded and the world spun about me. What would I do? The curse was back. Hadn't I paid the Universe everything! Would Joseph's ghost ruin Shelah's life too? Hadn't I given my pound of flesh and more?

'Thank you,' I muttered. 'You have done well. Please, have someone keep an eye on her family and let me know of anything that makes you think we can change her mind.'

My servant bowed. 'As you wish, my lord.'

Sleep evaded me that night. Phantoms and night visions of past sins haunted me. I dreamed of Er and Onan—my own flesh and blood that Heaven had struck down. My wife of twenty years stood before me, but was cold and out of reach. They circled to condemn me. Shadows passed in and out and proclaimed over me, 'Here is the life of the man who kills his brother!' Suddenly, I was in the pit—and Joseph stood, laughing over me as I cried for help.

The night faded into day. Everything was a daze and life was bitter. Shelah noticed and tried to find the source of my distress, but I didn't dare to tell him my sin had ruined his life. I was a coward. I couldn't look him in the eye and tell him that the inheritance wouldn't be his. He knew I was hiding something— but how could I tell my son that the sins of my youth would ensure his ruin? How could I tell him I'd murdered my brother and now his uncle's ghost would destroy his happy life?

For three days I walked as if dead. Waking and sleeping blurred together. All goodness and hope drifted out of my reach and those things which I'd put out of mind came back to proclaim their mastery over me. I'd planted the seeds of my condemnation as a young man, and twenty years later it was time to harvest. All was death and dark about me.

And, then, into my daze, came an unforeseen hope.

27

MY SERVANT RAN and kneeled before me.

'My lord, I have news!' he shouted, out of breath.

His greeting was an interruption to my cloud of self-pity and distress. He saw the confusion and distress on my face.

'My lord, I have news you'll want to know!'

'Nothing matters. Whatever news you carry, what difference can it make to a cursed man?'

My servant had never seen me in despair like this. 'But, my lord, this news could change a great deal.'

I raised my eyebrow. 'I doubt it. But go ahead.'

'My lord, Tamar is pregnant!'

I stared at my servant as if he was speaking a foreign language. His words made no sense to me.

'What?'

'Tamar, your daughter-in-law, the one you asked me to observe, it turns out she's pregnant. By the looks of it, she is quite far along.'

I knew this information was important, but it took a moment for me to appreciate the full implications.

'Who's the father?'

The servant fought back a grin. 'My lord, the girl is from a backwater Canaanite village. The father could be anyone.'

That's when it splashed on my face like a bucket of beer. 'She's pregnant? That's great! Do you know what this means?'

'My lord, it means by all the customs and traditions of our land that she's guilty of a great offence.'

'She should've waited for Shelah to bear his brother's son. She's an adulteress by local laws, correct?'

'Yes, my lord. It's custom to consider her an adulteress.'

'And the punishment of an adulteress is... what?'

'It depends on the circumstances. Local leaders decide.'

'Death?' I asked eagerly. 'I know adulteresses have been stoned before.'

My servant replied hesitantly, 'It would depend on the circumstances, my lord. A death penalty is rare and usually not considered necessary—but it's not unknown either.'

The oxygen of hope flooded my soul. Perhaps my son would have a life after all! This woman who had channelled Joseph's ghost and brought ruin to my home was guilty of a crime that could receive capital punishment—and I would ensure she received it. I would beat this devil. Heaven had seen my suffering and given me the tools to escape.

Was seeking her death harsh? Perhaps. But what was a parent to do? This was my son! I'd kept my hands blood-free since Joseph. I didn't want to be a violent man! But, if the only way my son could escape Joseph's curse was for this girl to die, then I'd strangle her with my own hands.

It wasn't hatred. It was the love of a father for his son that drove me to kill once again.

I didn't tell Shelah. I didn't wish to burden him and planned to inform him only after the fact. I gathered a group of scallywags and, with the lubricating help of alcohol and money, made a mob of them. Under the banner of justice, we'd slay an adulteress. I'd convinced them they were doing good for the wider community.

We left late morning. I wanted her dead by nightfall. The Canaanite belief was that fire could destroy the power of black magic and, though I was still Hebrew enough to reject such pagan superstition, I reasoned it couldn't hurt.

Walking with the men to her house took the whole day. I had plenty of time to reflect and change my mind. As I journeyed, an inconvenient truth knocked on the other side of the door of my conscience. Yes, I knew I wasn't planning on giving Shelah to Tamar anyway. So what? But that minor detail wasn't going to stop me from protecting my son.

'Tamar's to blame for everything that's happened! It was her fault my sons and wife died!' I repeated to myself as we walked through the pine forests and up to her village.

When we arrived that evening, the men circled the parents' house and the smaller house out back where Tamar lived. We knew she was inside. One of the younger men had run ahead to keep an eye on the property so that she wouldn't get an advanced warning and escape. We'd grab her, drag her away from the village, and then burn her.

One of my men called for her to come out.

We waited.

Then, after a few moments, the strangest thing happened. A girl came out. Not a young woman, like Tamar. But a child. She came out of Tamar's home carrying a small box. Trembling, she approached one of the men and addressed him.

I was curious. Was she carrying a plea for mercy from Tamar? Was there money in the box? I'd already determined not to tolerate any pleading or bargaining. I'd close my ears to her screams. I'd hardened my heart to kill Joseph. I'd do it again.

The man led the girl to me. 'She has something for you, Judah.'

I stared at her. 'What is this, child?'

'It's from my mistress, my lord.'

'Is she pleading for her life?'

'No, my lord. She wants to give you the contents of this box.'

'Ha! What is it? A pittance of gold?' Does she think she can save her life through bribery? Give it to me!' I commanded.

The child handed the box over.

I felt its weight. Pine. The wood was and contents seemed light. 'You, with the torch, come over here. I need some light.'

'Was there any message from your mistress to go with it?'

'Yes, my lord. She wanted me to ask "Do these look familiar? Do you know who they belong to?"'

A chill shot through me. 'What did you just say?'

"Do these look familiar? Do you know who they belong to?"

Those words seemed strangely familiar, like questions from a bad dream long before. My father's face and a bloodied robe passed before my mind's eye. My hand trembled as I grabbed hold of the box's lid and lifted it. I peered inside.

'Bring the torch closer!' I barked. I gazed inside.

It *was* something familiar. I looked closer.

Then I dropped the box and a blankness enveloped me. Myself, my I, was blown away like ashes in the wind.

Inside were my ring and cord.

I was the father.

28

OLIVER STARED ACROSS the table as his mind raced with questions. Judah turned to Tamar and Tamar returned his gaze. She tapped her painted nails against a now empty coffee mug.

Oliver wasn't sure who to address, so he asked his question out loud, 'The fact that it was your stuff in the box means—'

'Yep,' Tamar interrupted. 'That's what it means.'

'So, when he went up to the mountains to party, that meant you were the—'

'The whore? Yeah. *C'est moi.* I dressed up, knocked his boots off, and took his stuff," she said, matter-of-factly, with neither pride nor shame.

He looked at Judah. 'You slept with your daughter-in-law?'

'I didn't do any sleeping.'

Oliver closed his eyes. 'You. Know. What. I. Mean.'

Judah nodded. 'I didn't know it was her. The tent was dark and she wore a pretty veil.'

Tamar smiled. 'You liked that veil?'

'It was lovely.'

Tamar rolled her shoulders 'Ah, thanks! I'll have to remember that next time I go out with the girls. They'll—'

'Guys!' Oliver interrupted. 'Who cares about the veil? What you're describing is an absolute mess—daytime TV talk show kinda mess. How can you live with yourselves?'

'First of all, we're dead,' Judah replied. 'The redeemed have no shame in the second life. Secondly, as I said, I didn't know. I did many evil deeds during my life on earth, but intentionally sleeping with a girl meant for my son wasn't one of them.'

'OK, I suppose you can't be fully blamed,' Oliver conceded. 'But what happened after you found out? You didn't burn her, did you?'

'Correct deduction. Opening that box was a turning point in my life. When I realised the items in that box were mine, my life began to change. The fortress of justifications and excuses I'd built up over the years received a mighty blow. It was as if a voice spoke to me from the box, crying: *You are the man!* It rocked me like an earthquake right in front of the other men.

'Did they know what was happening?' Oliver asked.

'No. They didn't understand. Several minutes passed before I was able to articulate the words I needed to call them off and send them home. During that time I lay, face in the dust, grabbing my sides and groaning.'

Oliver looked at Tamar. 'Were you inside all this time?'

'Yep. Watching it all from the window.'

'How'd you know how Judah would respond?'

'I didn't. I took a chance. But that's how badly I wanted this. Yes, money was part of it. Judah's pay off was small compared to the wealth I'd have as the matriarch. But there was also the significance. Getting to know Judah's family showed me that there was something different about them—and I was desperate for different.'

Oliver turned to Judah. 'What happened then?'

'After I pulled myself off the ground, I paid and dismissed the men and headed home. In the days that followed, the way I saw the world began to change. Before I'd run from guilt and blamed others whenever things didn't work out. I'd blamed my father, Joseph, Tamar, or God for my problems. But, when I opened that box, I realised that all my problems had one common denominator: me. I was responsible for them.'

'But,' Oliver interjected, 'When you spoke earlier, you didn't strike me as having been lazy or irresponsible.'

'In one sense, no, I wasn't. I was a hard worker and one that others trusted to get jobs done. I was competent in business. But in my relationships and personal behaviour, it was a different matter. My hurts had turned a dark shade of bitter and accusations had become like breathing. I saw others as "the bad guy". That shifting of blame led me to believe Tamar had carried a curse into our family. That's why I tried to murder her.

'It had been the same for Joseph. My father's blatant favouritism cut deep. But instead of acknowledging my need for love, I wounded others as my father had wounded me. I blamed Tamar and Joseph, but they were more righteous than I.'

'It was like he became a new fella after all this—and I got to see it all up close,' Tamar chimed in.

'What happened to you?' Oliver asked.

'I moved back in with Judah, Shelah, and the fam. I gave birth to twin boys.'

'Really? Did you marry Shelah?'

'No, I never married again. But my eldest boy was now set to inherit from Judah in the name of my husband, Er. I was the unmarried matriarch to be.'

'We never slept together again,' Judah interjected. 'But we did become friends and raised the twins together.'

'You're a weird pair.'

Judah continued. 'Then we moved back in with my family.'

'Your dad and brothers?

'Yes.'

'Wow, after twenty years you returned?'

'Indeed. Putting aside pride and humbling yourself changes how you see both yourself and others. Now, when I looked at my dad, I no longer saw a cruel monster. Rather, he was a broken man with broken children.'

'That's one messed up story—yet one with a strangely satisfying resolution.'

'That may have been the end of one of life's chapters, but the story is not done. Not yet. In this world, there is always more story. Some just get stuck in the same chapter.'

'Why do I feel you're gonna talk about me now?'

Tamar lit another cigarette. 'Oli-vuh, we're here to help ya go forward. Ya got a destiny. But ya can't step into it as ya are.'

Oliver sighed. 'This again? Why should I even listen to you two? As interesting as your stories are, you can't be anything more than a hallucination or strange dream.'

Judah sipped his bourbon. 'Why do you say that?'

'Because I believe in science and I'm ninety-nine percent certain that there's no such thing as angels, aliens, miracles, or the paranormal.'

Tamar smirked. 'That one percent's a real kick in the balls, ain't it?'

Oliver grinned. 'OK, you got me. I can't prove there's nothing beyond the material world. I'm just, I dunno, sceptical.'

Tamar reached across the table and laid her warm and solid hand on Oliver's. 'Then forget whatever ya think we are or are not. Just hear our message.'

'Before a man can receive mercy from heaven,' Judah said, 'He must learn an important truth: my life is my responsibility. When you stop seeing yourself as the good guy and those around you as the bad guys who are to blame for your problems, then you can move forward.'

Oliver squirmed. 'But sometimes things are the fault of employers, parents, or the government, right? Sometimes we are victims. Should I deny I've had problems thrown my way?'

'Sure, you've had problems—so has everyone,' Judah replied. 'But being a victim doesn't make you more righteous. Suffering under my dad's favouritism made me bitter, not better. You are not always responsible for what happens to you, but you are always response-able.'

Oliver kicked back. 'So my problems are still my fault?'

'No. But just because something's not your fault, doesn't mean it's not your responsibility. True men don't waste their lives complaining about how hard or unfair everything is.'

Oliver cast a doubtful glare. 'Is that what it means to be a man? Excuse me, I wasn't aware that, beyond physiology, there was a set definition to manhood.'

'Oh, yes,' Judah retorted. 'I know it's not popular in this day to think so, but true masculinity involves the joyful acceptance of responsibility. It's an honour, not just a burden. When you lead, you assume responsibility for things that aren't your fault.'

'Yes, it's important to be responsible,' Oliver conceded. 'But, in a broken system like ours, can't men also be victims?

Tamar puffed out a cloud of smoke. 'Course they can be, Oli-vuh. Men suffer tragedy all the time. So do women. But if ya think the system in Britain is more broken than others, ya don't get out much.'

'Well, yes, I suppose it could be worse.'

'Ya see, I did some nasty things and had nasty things were happenin' to me. Everyone has nasty things happen to them. The question is, whatcha gonna do about it? Ya gonna spend ya whole life blamin' others and blamin' the system? Or, are ya gonna man up and do the best ya can with what ya got? Lots of men blame their crappy lives on others—and they go nowhere.'

Oliver had a retort all ready to explain why he wasn't such a man—but then he paused. The image of Elise, with tear flowing down her cheek, hovered back into his mind. He could argue and make excuses with Judah and Tamar, but it was still his irresponsibility that had hurt the purest girl he knew.

'I-I guess I'm one of those men you describe,' he said and planted his face into his folded arms on the table. 'I need help.'

Tamar, who was still holding his hand, squeezed it. Oliver lifted his head. 'Elise deserves to be with a real man. I'd like to be one, but the process doesn't sound comfortable.'

'Alotta men are addicted to their comfort. We're here to give ya resources to grow. But first, there's more story ya must hear.'

'I thought the curse was broken. Wasn't it?'

Judah nodded. 'The root power of the curse had been struck, and Heaven was giving me mercy to become a new man. But I still needed to undo the deeds of my past. I had to face my ghost. This time as a whole man.'

'How'd you do that?'

'It began back at my father's house. But it didn't end there.'

29

'O-OK. LET ME get this straight,' Levi said, tearing up with laughter. 'Y-you thought she was a p-prostitute?'

'Laugh it up, moron!' I yelled.

'I-I don't know what's stupider,' he laughed, 'G-getting seduced by your daughter-in-law, or, or giving a prostitute your cord and ring!'

'Shut! Up!'

He rolled in fits of hysterics. 'So now, your - your kids are also-also your grandkids! That's priceless!' he roared.

It had been many years since I'd punched Levi. But I made up for the lost time.

My brothers slaughtered a fattened calf as part of my welcome home party. They'd visited me while I was in self-exile, but there's nothing like being home. They also welcomed Shelah and the rest of the family. A few, like Levi, rolled their eyes over the situation with Tamar and the twins but, having grown up with four mothers, we were used to dysfunctions.

Father also welcomed me, but he was a shell of the man he'd once been. He'd never recovered from Joseph's death. Now that I was home, I desired to build up the family—and he was willing to let me try.

The year I moved back, however, famine struck. At first, we thought it was just a bad, local harvest. But as our servants journeyed to other lands, we realised that this famine was global. Crops dried up everywhere. Of course, we had grain reserves and assumed it was just a bad year. Nothing more.

But then the second year came and the crops failed again. They failed everywhere. We'd never encountered a situation like this. Our supplies were nearly gone and we were anxious. My brothers looked to me for guidance, but I had no answers.

Then we got word that Egypt had stores of grain. Somehow they were ready for all this—so we prepared for a trip down south.

Dad kept our youngest brother, Benjamin, behind. He was Rachel's second son, the one she'd died in childbirth with, and therefore the new Joseph. My dad was still my dad—shortcomings and all. At first, I feared I might despise Benjamin as I had Joseph. But I didn't. The hatred just wasn't there this time. My pride was no longer big enough to be wounded. How could I blame my dad for what he did with his son? I almost murdered Tamar to protect my boy! I wasn't in a position to judge another father.

We took donkeys with us to bring back as much Egyptian grain as possible. The mission was meant to be short and simple. The trip down was fun and easy-going. But, when we arrived two weeks later, everything collapsed.

The city was grander than anything we had ever seen. All the little towns of Canaan were a backwater by comparison. The buildings, temples, and statues stole our breath away.

It was crowded. The whole world was seeking food there and we waited for hours in the queue just to buy grain. As we approached the front, a grand persona stepped off his lofty seat. The soldiers indicated with spears that we should bow.

'Where do you come from?' he shouted through a translator.

'We're from Canaan. We've come to buy food,' we replied, the translator relaying our words to him in Egyptian.

Everything about this man was efficient and serious. His gaze caused us to quake. It was the type of stare that isn't wondering *if* you're guilty of evil—only *what* evil you've done. To our horror, he scowled and pointed straight at us.

'Spies! You've come to discover our weaknesses!' he shouted.

We trembled, unsure of what to say. Simeon was the first to find his words. 'No, Your Excellency. We're sons of one man— brothers. We're not spies!'

The Viceroy raged on. 'Ha! All from one man? You're spies!'

At this, we fell on our knees and soldiers surrounded us. We pleaded, 'No, Your Excellency. Our father had twelve sons in all. One has died. The youngest is with our father in Canaan.'

'I don't believe you!' he yelled. 'But I'll give you a chance to prove your innocence. One of you must go back home and bring your brother to me. Then I'll consider you trustworthy!'

Then, soldiers dragged us off to a damp Egyptian prison. Our minds raced, trying to make sense of what had happened. 'Why would he think we're spies?' we asked one another. Our hearts began to slow back down as the true nightmare of our situation dawned on us. Each of us dealt with the trauma in his own way.

'You should've let me do the talking!' Reuben complained.

'We need a plan. Gather up, let's hear your ideas,' I ordered.

Then there was Levi. 'Hello, guard? I like my morning baths warm but not too hot. Three poached eggs and bread fried in butter should do it for breakfast. Don't wake me before eight. Oh, and please bring me an extra pillow, thanks.'

I wouldn't have even kept my sheep in the nasty cell they crammed us into. We ate little and slept less. We discussed who should return to dad and how that person might take more than one donkey loaded with food so that our families wouldn't starve.

After three days, and without warning, the soldiers took us out of our cell. They surrounded us with their spears and herded us back to the Viceroy. When we approached, he rose from his throne and came near. As we bowed in respect he said, 'I've reconsidered.' He was calmer than before. 'I fear Heaven and wouldn't want your agéd father to go without food. You're free to return. I'll only keep one of you back. I'll set him free and sell you more food when you return with your youngest. Do you understand?'

'Yes, your Excellency,' we replied in thankful submission. We hated the idea of leaving even one of us behind but, still, this was an improvement. Plus, we had no choice.

'Why's this happening?' one of us asked.

'Isn't it obvious?'

'Not to me.'

'We murdered our brother by sending him to Egypt. Now fate makes us suffer for it here.'

Reuben was unhelpful as ever. 'I told you so! Told you we shouldn't have harmed him! We're only in this mess because you never listen to me. And I'm the oldest!'

After Reuben's outburst, a silence swept over the room. We'd never spoken about what happened in those hills so many years earlier. We'd privately thought of it—but never dared speak of it aloud. We'd tried to forget our fratricide. Of course, the memory had terrorized me for years. But I'd assumed that, since I was the one who led the brothers to sell Joseph, it was only I who'd face the curse.

The Viceroy chose Simeon to stay behind. He allowed the rest of us to buy grain. We paid for it, loaded up our donkeys, and headed for home. But, on the way back, something happened that turned our stomachs.

We stopped for the night. One of us began to make a fire while three others went searching for wood. Gad opened his sack to get some grain for roasting.

That's when he started screaming.

We ran to see what it was. We looked at Gad's hands—he was grasping onto something. I recognized what it was and gasped.

It was the money we'd given the Egyptians.

My jaw dropped. 'It can't be!' several of us muttered.

The curse was upon us all.

30

WE GATHERED AROUND the sack of grain and stared at the money. All at once, fear-fuelled words fired from their mouths.

'How's this possible? Didn't you pay the man?'

'Of course, I paid!'

'Then why's the money in your bag?'

'I don't know! Why's any of this happening?'

'The Egyptians will kill us for stealing!"

'It's Joseph's ghost seeking revenge!'

'We'll die for our guilt!'

'Must our families also suffer?'

My brothers expressed the same anxieties that had been my regular companions ever since Er died. Instead of this curse being satisfied, it hungered for my whole family—as if I'd brought death home with me and infected everyone. Fear robbed me of sleep that night. Guilt weighed heavy as I mused the possibility that I'd brought a malediction upon everyone I'd ever loved.

We arrived home and told our dad everything. He didn't know what to make of it any more than we had. When we told him the Viceroy demanded to see Benjamin, he shuddered.

When we put our grain in storage, things got even stranger. We opened our bags and we found money in each one! All of it in our sacks! My dad's hand trembled as he touched the silver. He spun towards us, madness in his eyes.

'What's this? When you return, they'll imprison you as thieves. You can't take Benjamin. I, I won't let you! He's mine! My son! I lost Joseph. Now Simeon. I won't lose Benjamin too!'

'You can trust Benjamin with me, dad.' Reuben piped up with as much heroics as he could muster. 'If I don't bring him back safely, you can kill both my sons yourself!'

Father sighed—Rueben was always trying to seem capable without actually being capable. Then he looked at the rest of us. 'Why do these things happen to me? Why does life continue to rain darkness on me? No! I Benjamin is all I've left of Rachel. This food will have to last.'

And, with that, he sulked back to his tent.

**

Nine months later, our stomachs ached and our bodies grew thin. As our family business was based on sheep and cattle, we'd fed a lot of our grain to the animals to keep them alive—that's how scarce grass was. We knew we were dying, but none of us knew what to do about it.

I'd seen my wife and two sons die while in exile. I never thought I'd see my brothers pass away too. But the spectre of death was near—and I had a front-row seat to its devastating performance.

The tragedy of the situation was that it was so unnecessary. That's what broke me. Our father, once so great and mighty in our eyes, had shrivelled. The one who'd wrestled an angel and faced down Esau was hiding in his tent? He was pitiful, and his obsession with his youngest son was causing all of us, including that son, to slowly die. We knew we needed to change his mind—but he was the patriarch! Confronting him over his failures required more courage than any of us had.

It was Tamar that gave me the kick I needed.

'Here's all the grain we have until next week,' I said one evening, dropping two bags at the entrance to her tent.

She stepped outside and looked down at the bags. 'This is it for five days? You, Shelah, me, the twins, and the servants?'

'Our whole household,' I said grimly.

'To think I once married into this family for wealth! Ha! Whadda ya think of that? Life's got a dark sense of humour.'

'That it does.'

'Who's gonna fast this week?'

'The twins need their food. The servants work hard in the sun. They'll faint without it. Shelah and I can both skip a day.'

Tamar folded her arms. 'I'll miss one too then.'

'Thanks,' I said with a grin. 'Welcome to our family. Hope it's everything you dreamed.'

'What more could a girl want, eh?'

I looked down at her feet, feeling ashamed that I couldn't provide more for my children. 'I'm sorry, Tamar. Truly. For everything.'

She put her hand on my shoulder. 'Hey, what's this? Don't get all soft now big guy. Listen, this ain't your fault. But ...'

'Yeah?'

'But there's something ya can do.'

My gaze met hers. 'Yeah?'

'Look, ya the leader here. Everyone knows it. When ya pop goes, who else do all these brothers look to? If anyone can talk him into releasin' Benjamin, it's you.'

'My dad loves Benjamin. He'll never let him go.'

'I love Benji too! Heck, I don't know how ya even have a brother as great as him.'

I laughed. 'Touché.'

'Benji's one of the reasons I'm here. But that great lil' brother is gonna die just like Shelah, the twins, and all the rest of us if we don't get some food.'

'What do you suggest?'

'Whaddo I suggest? Man-up, big guy! I know how much yous respect your father—and good on you for doing so. But he's still lost in grief over that dead brother of yours from long ago.'

I squirmed and turned my gaze aside. 'Yeah ... there's that.'

'There's only one of yous that your father respects enough to listen to. That's you.'

'Hm, I suppose so.'

'I know so.'

'What do you think I should say?'

'How should I know? Ya the man—our future leader. Come up with somethin' and make it convincin'!'

I smiled at her. 'So Heaven gives me daughter-in-law who thinks she's my mum?'

She winked back. 'One does one's best.'

'OK. I'll try it—soon.'

I knew persuading my dad would involve opening up to him. I'd have to look him in the eyes and pour out my heart. But would even that work? What if I pleaded with him and he rebuked me for suggesting he risk Benjamin?

The thought of such a rejection would've once broken me. But now things were different. I was different. And I wasn't doing this for me—I was doing this for my family. I was even doing it for my dad. He was once a great man, but his nostalgic obsession was killing him. Literally and spiritually.

My opportunity came over dinner one evening. It was another of our pitiful meals. The days of plenty of wine and cheese were only memories. Meat now had to be rationed. We were forced to eat mostly bread and vegetables—and even they were getting low.

Father slapped his cup of water from the table and yelled, 'Why doesn't one of you go to Egypt for food? Huh? We'll starve if this continues!'

Our bodies snapped to attention. The table went silent. We looked at each other—shaking our heads. How could he ask this? How could he ask the impossible? How could he send any of us to Egypt, knowing they'd imprison whoever went?

My brothers were silent. Our father's request was a mockery. But I saw my opportunity. I stood and bowed before my father before making eye contact. 'Father, you know why we can't do that. The Viceroy said we wouldn't be allowed to buy anything from him unless we return with our brother.'

His eyes flashed. 'Why'd you do that, huh? Why'd you tell him you have a little brother? You wanna break my heart?'

He was completely self-absorbed. My jaw tightened. I fought to suppress the scream growing within me. How was he so blind? How could a man blame others while he destroyed them?

I knew how. I'd been that man.

I took a deep breath. 'Dad, we didn't know the Viceroy would imprison Simeon or demand Benjamin. Is blaming us fair? He simply asked questions about where we came from.'

My father was listening.

'Dad, entrust the boy to me,' I pleaded. 'I know what it's like to lose a son. I've lost two! You can't hold onto Benjamin like this. It will result in his death as well as ours.'

A tear trickled down my dad's cheek. 'Let go of the boy,' I said. 'I'll be accountable before you if I lose him. I won't blame anyone. It'll be my fault alone. I can't promise his safety. But I know, from experience, what losing him would mean to you.'

When I finished speaking, no one moved.

Then my buried his face in his hands and began to sob. The rest of us watched, without speaking or moving. Finally, he lifted his head, returned my gaze, and nodded.

Then I spoke a hard truth. One that he needed to hear for this to work. 'Dad, if you hadn't held onto Benjamin this long, we could've gone down and been back twice by now.' My father knew what that implied. He needed to own the situation.

Silence weighed down on us like a cloud. Would he release Benjamin? We dared not breathe as we waited for his response.

'You're right,' he finally said. 'I won't pretend. Judah, I entrust—,' he paused mid-sentence. 'm-my son to you.'

'Thank you. I will do my best.'

'I know,' he replied. Then he stood and breathed deeply. He opened his mouth and began to command in a way that none of us had heard in a long time. 'Gather nuts and honey! Get some of the best produce of the land. Be smart! Take double the silver with you and offer it as soon as you arrive—before the Egyptians can even bring the matter up of the missing money. Show them we're not thieves. We are the sons of Abraham and Isaac—we'll give no room for accusations against our character!'

As he spoke, my father's voice rose loud and clear and we saw the man we'd known in our youth. His eyes shown with light. His chin was up. He paced to and fro—without his walking stick. He knew his family was at risk and he spoke with wisdom on how to navigate the potential pitfalls of our journey.

Our pulses raced. Our eyes danced. Joy filled the atmosphere. The man who'd withered away while nursing self-pity had stepped out of his cave. Our father had come back into the sunlight of life. The energy of his presence filled the room and imparted vigour to everyone. Israel was back!

By the grace of Heaven, I'd rescued my dad.

31

WE STRODE OFF towards Egypt with our shoulders back and chins up. It was a new day. We were the sons of Israel, equipped with our dad's wisdom and blessing.

If only we'd known what lay ahead.

As the days and miles flowed by, the gravity of the situation weighed increasingly upon us. The man we'd present Benjamin reigned with nearly unlimited authority. What if he didn't accept our gifts or believe our story about the money? A word from his mouth could slay us.

Still, we carried clean consciences and had considered carefully our plan.

When we arrived in the capital, a servant alerted the Viceroy of our presence. Later, he returned to inform us, to our great surprise, that we'd be eating at the Viceroy's home.

Nothing could have prepared us adequately for such an experience! It was a banquet like none we'd had in Canaan. We were escorted into a grand room with tables full of fine Egyptian foods and wines. Musicians played beautiful music on instruments I'd never even heard of before. Simeon was also reunited with us at this time amidst hugs and laughter.

But that afternoon was as strange as it was delicious. When we explained about the silver in our sacks, the Viceroy dismissed it. He told us to keep our money. He then devolved into quite an emotional state when we presented Benjamin to him. What's more, his servants served Benjamin far more food than us. In the old days, we would've complained over him being favoured or talked about "fairness". Our envy would've ruined it. But, as we all had plenty, we were happy for him— only curious as to why he was singled out.

The Viceroy and the Egyptians dinned at another table. To them, Canaanites are unclean and not to be eaten with. But we cared little about the discrimination. We had food in our bellies and they hadn't imprisoned us like last time! We didn't complain that the world wasn't perfect as our younger selves would've done. We simply enjoyed the moment.

The next day we expressed our gratitude to the Viceroy and his ministers and set out for home. Our donkeys were loaded and we were aquiver with eagerness to tell our dad of all our good fortune. It had been almost a year since Simeon had been home and he was eager to see his wife and children. I too was eager to get home—not least of all that I might present Benjamin back to my dad. Though he'd made the decision to entrust the boy to me, I knew he was nervous. I imagined him hiking up a hill and peering south each day to see if he could spot us on the horizon. That's what I would've done for Shelah or the twins.

But then, it all fell apart.

32

WE HAD JOURNEYED an hour from Egypt's capital when a rumble grew behind us. To our horror, an Egyptian cavalry was galloping straight towards us! They circled and drew their swords at us. We screamed, thinking they'd chop us down that very instant. What was this?

An official got down from his horse. We recognised him as the Viceroy's steward. Fire was in his eyes and fury on his face—and we cowered before him.

'Why do you repay good with evil?' he shouted. 'Why did you steal my master's magical goblet? You sons of wickedness, did you think we wouldn't notice? Theives!'

We looked around at each other but saw only confusion mirrored in every face.

One of the brothers spoke. 'Why do you say these things? Didn't we bring back the money we found in our sacks last time? We are not thieves! If you find the cup, you may kill that man—and enslave the rest of us!'

The steward sneered. 'Keep your bravado! We'll only take the one who stole the cup. We don't need any more stinking Canaanite sheepherders as slaves.'

'We don't have it,' my brother shot back. 'None of us do!'

The rest of us nodded.

Then I spoke up. 'Sir, my brothers and I are far from perfect, but stealing a magic cup to communicate with your Egyptian gods isn't our schtick. There's no way any of us would put our journey at risk by stealing—especially from someone as grand as your master.'

'We'll see,' he retorted back. 'Soldiers, search them!'

The soldiers began to examine our donkeys and luggage. They started with the oldest brother and worked towards the youngest. We denied their accusation, but our objections fell on deaf ears. As they searched, I couldn't shake the fear that Joseph's ghost hadn't yet consumed his whole pound of flesh.

But then, the unthinkable happened. When the soldiers reached the final donkey, they opened the sack and there lay the Viceroy's cup!

'No!' I cried. 'Not him!'

We fell to our feet and pleaded but the soldiers commanded us to our feet and marched us back to the city.

I looked up to Heaven. 'Why Benjamin? Will my dad's heart be broken again? Will I be guilty before him of losing yet another favourite son? Why don't you stop this? Will my sufferings never atone for the sins of my youth?'

We arrived back in the capital at dusk—just as the sun was bathing the city in a urine yellow hue. They dragged us to the Viceroy's throne where soldiers surrounded us.

'Why'd you steal from me?' both he and his translator roared. 'You should've known a man of my quality can wield supernatural divination and command spirits! Did you think I wouldn't notice?'

We were speechless, trapped in a nightmare. I stepped forward and opened my mouth before the words, spinning wildly in my head, had solidified into sentences.

'Y-your Excellency,' I stuttered. 'What can I say? I don't know how to answer this accusation, I don't know how this has happened. Heaven has exposed my sin and the sin of my brothers. We are your slaves.'

The Viceroy squinted and stared into my soul. I trembled, but not because I was a good man who had met a bad ruler. I was a guilty man who was laying before the face of final justice—and the rightness of it shook the core of me.

'No!' he shouted. 'I'll do no such thing. I don't punish the innocent. We'll only enslave the man who stole the goblet. The rest may go back home. You're innocent.'

For the second time in my life, the destiny of my favoured little brother was in my hands. Last time I'd disposed of that brother for my own sake. But now? No. I knew what I must do. Last time, I sacrificed my little brother for myself.

This time, I'd sacrifice myself for my little brother.

'Excuse me, Your Excellency!' I said, coming closer to the Viceroy. The soldiers stepped forward, drawing their swords.

The Viceroy roared in the Egyptian tongue and the soldiers stepped back. I fell on my knees before him.

'Please, Your Excellency. Allow me to speak and don't be angry. My dad, your servant, allowed this boy to come down with us under my care. He's the second son of his favourite wife. The first son died and now the soul of my dad is wrapped up with this boy's welfare. If I return without him, my dad will die in misery. Please don't cause me to pierce my dad's heart with sorrow beyond measure.'

The Viceroy's eyes blazed down upon me. 'What would you have me do? He stole from me! Should I ignore justice?'

'Take me as a replacement instead.'

The room fell silent. 'What'd you say?' he asked.

'Please, Your Excellency, take me! Let me be his replacement as your slave. Yes, I'm older, but ask my brothers—they'll testify that I'm a hard and competent worker.

The Viceroy was noticeably shocked by the proposal. 'You'd substitute your free life for his condemned life?'

'Yes, Your Excellency. Replace his life with mine. Let his guilt fall on me. Let my life atone for his sin.'

My body convulsed as the words poured from my soul onto his feet like water. 'Please, I'll no longer fight to keep my life. I freely give it to Your Excellency in my brother's stead.'

And, with that, my words were finished. I committed myself to Heaven and prayed the Viceroy would accept the exchange.

Finally, he spoke. 'Servants, soldiers, leave us!' Their feet scurried across the floor and out of the room.

And we were all alone with this Prince of Egypt.

I was still kneeling at his feet when the howl erupted. His scream exploded from his gut like when a man is about to die— or learns his son has died. His tears fell on my hands.

'Is it magic? Is he conjuring a spirit or another curse?' I asked myself in a whisper.

Then my body jolted in surprise—his hand had grabbed my hair and he was pulling me up. His howl came to an end. His wild and tortured face was just inches from mine.

What is this madness! I thought that my life was going to end. *Will he stab me with his knife or speak a word of Egyptian magic that'll end my life on the spot?*

He opened his mouth and breathed deeply.

'Do your worst! I deserved it. Just show my brother mercy!'

He nodded at my words as if he understood.

Then he smiled.

Then he spoke.

When he spoke—how can I describe it?—he might as well as have struck me in the face with his sceptre. Words that I could never have anticipated ripped my spine right out of my backbone. They tore like the claws of a thousand animals pulling me out of my skin. The curse that I'd battled for years ripped my soul like a curtain torn from top to bottom. It simultaneously destroyed me and liberated me.

I heard the ghost speak.

'It's me, Joseph.'

33

OLIVER LEAPT FROM his chair. 'No!'

Judah looked back at him and nodded. 'Yes, Mr Anderson. And so it was.'

'But, how?' Oliver sputtered in unbelief. 'W-was it his ghost incarnate in the Viceroy? Was he speaking from beyond the grave? What did he do to you? Execute justice?'

'On that day, my haunting was complete. All I had sowed in the soil of life, I finally reaped. It had come full circle. My real brother faced me in the flesh. He'd not died in Egypt after all.'

'The brother you sold? How does a slave become Viceroy?'

'It's a long story—enough to say that Heaven was with him.'

'What happened next? Did he try to kill you?'

'Let's just say, the experience killed the old Judah once and for all. At that moment, I died.'

Oliver's mind swirled with questions. 'But, how? I can't imagine how it must feel to face justice twenty years later!'

Judah rubbed his beard. 'We all eventually reap what we sow. Our Universe is woven through with justice. Your life is no different. Eventually, you'll face the consequences of your decisions. Some you'll face sooner, some later.'

'Well, I've never trafficked anyone. There's no way I'd ever face a consequence so dramatic.'

'The chains we put Joseph in were on the outside. The chains I crafted for myself were on the inside—and it took a power greater than myself to be liberated.'

'It's like that for everybody,' Tamar added. 'The place ya give to envy and lies will haunt ya. Even what ya call white lies can be monstrous later on.'

Oliver bristled. 'Whoa—I want to hear what happened to Judah and his brothers. Why is this suddenly about me again?'

'That's why we're here. We're not like one of your daytime TV shows where a perky female and a tamed, beta-male chit-chat with celebrities and tell heart-warming stories. We came here to tell you the truth, even if it's hard to hear.'

Tamar took off her sunglasses. 'Remember, we've come—'

'To help me,' Oliver groaned. 'Yeah, so you keep saying. But what I—' he began to protest, but he stopped short when he noticed Tamar's eyes—Judah's too. It struck him how they radiated life. He'd always imagined that, if ghosts existed, their eyes would be cold and dead. But the eyes staring at him now were packed with more purpose and meaning than any he'd ever seen—certainly more than the two he saw each day in the mirror.

'Ya was sayin' somethin' Oli-vuh?'

'I-I don't think it was so important.'

'Ya wanna continue?'

'Yes, please,' Oliver affirmed, regaining his thoughts. 'Judah, you spoke a moment ago about the Universe and justice. What did you mean exactly?'

'Simply that, in the end, none of us gets away with anything. Everyone will be haunted. The only question is: what will you do with their haunting? Will you travel further into the darkness or overcome it? We all have a day of reckoning where we'll sit down to a banquet of hellish consequences.'

Oliver scowled at that word. 'What's that supposed to mean? If I don't live right and repent, I'm going to hell?'

Tamar puffed out her cigarette. 'Pffh? Ya think the angels are gonna take your scrawny behind to the ice cream parlour?'

'Let me put it this way' Judah resumed, 'When you chose darkness over light, your life—in both time and eternity—becomes more hellish. But a haunted man can still be redeemed. If you choose wisely, you can die before you die.'

At the mention of death, Oliver flinched. 'Huh? Die?'

'When the ghosts come, make them ya guides,' Tamar said.

'Wait—what? Now you're purposefully playing with me. How can ghosts guide me? I thought ghosts were bad?'

'When we do evil, our consequences pursue us,' Judah said. 'They're a type of judgment—but judgments can be used for good, even if they terrify and break us.'

'What good can judgment do?'

Tamar smiled. 'Every lesson a ghost teaches leads to a destination—truths ya must face. It's living those truths that'll grow ya into a man.'

Oliver shook his head. 'You've already shown me plenty of truth—especially about how my behaviour is hurting Elise. What bigger truth about being a man do I need to face?'

Tamar and Judah looked at each other, smiled, and then turned back to Oliver. 'How to die,' they said in unison.

Oliver's stomach turned. 'You said that a moment ago.'

'And we'll keep saying it until you understand,' Judah said.

'What, you're my parents now? Is this what I'm supposed to learn?' Oliver's frustration resurged. 'Why would I want to die? I wanna live! You've got to *carpe* the ol' *diem* while you can!'

Judah wasn't intimidated by Oliver's angst. 'This life is your only chance to die, Mr Anderson. After this, you must live forever with who you are.'

The idea of living forever, as he was, made Oliver's heart jump—though he hardly knew why. 'What? Now you're speaking in riddles—morbid ones at that.'

'Oliv-uh, sweetheart, we know ya wanna live, but ya can't live until you die. Not truly.'

'Die to live?'

'Perhaps someone else should explain this,' Judah replied.

'Huh? Someone else? No! First of all, I'm not sure I want to understand this. Secondly, you two are more than enough for one night. If you have some other phantom waiting in the next room, tell them to stay. Your stories have been fascinating, but I must draw the line when you start talking about my death.'

Judah smiled. 'You have a choice. Do you remember why I came over here? You told Tamar you wanted a lift to the manor where the band is waiting.'

The band? Oliver had completely forgotten. 'Yes, of course! Where has my mind been?'

Judah continued. 'You have a choice. You can get into my truck and I can take you there now, or you can meet someone who will explain why you must die.'

'The choices you offer always feel like a whack from an angry ex-girlfriend. I want this nightmare done! I wanna do what I came into the countryside to do. Your stories have been interesting—book worthy even. Some of your advice about responsibility and women hasn't been half-bad. But you've gotten weird now—and meeting another of weirdo won't help.'

'If this is your choice, we will respect it. But I cannot promise that you will ever have this opportunity again. Once this night is through, the door may be closed forever.'

Oliver paused. As annoyed as he was at Judah and Tamar making their stories about him, he knew they had some wisdom—even if it was irritating at times.

'Who, exactly, will finish explaining if not you two?'

Judah shook his head. 'When we open ourselves to the truth, we never get to know what channels it might come through.'

'Could he or she come in the truck and explain on the way?'

All Oliver got in response to this suggestion was the sound of Judah clearing his throat and raised eyebrows from Tamar. He may as well have asked the seasons to move for his convenience.

Oliver sighed and stared down at the table. He hated choices. *I've already learnt enough to fix things up with Elise. I'm sure I could read about these things later in a good book or learn them from my grandfather.* The room was silent as Oliver's mind waded through his valley of decision. *I've already lost several hours, if I hurry, I can still get some footage with the band.*

Finally, Oliver looked up. 'OK, here's what I want. I've chosen to—'

But Oliver never finished his sentence. Suddenly the room shook and the table leapt.

Oliver jumped out of his seat. 'W-what the … an earthquake? But this is England!'

Judah nodded. 'You've made your choice, Mr Anderson.'

Tamar placed her hand to her lips and blew a kiss. 'Good-bye, Oliv-uh. It's been swell. I hope to see ya again.'

And with that, the room began to fade.

'Stop it! What's happening' The room became colder. Oliver felt a draft blow over him. He looked across the table—Judah and Tamar were melting away. The whole room became less opaque as if he could see through it. He felt the vibrating floor begin to give way.

'Help, I'm, sinking!' he shouted.

Then, a gust of wind blew past and took the house away as if it were made of tissue paper. He fell and slammed into the wet earth.

34

OLIVER GROANED. HE lay on the cold ground while the wind howled above him. He rubbed his head, sore from the fall. Finally, he sat up and looked around. There was no trace of a house, a car, or another living soul. His jacket was on the ground fifteen feet away. He sprang up, rushed over to it, and wrapped it around him from the cold and wind.

'Judah? Tamar?' Oliver called, but his voice was lost in the wind and the emptiness of the countryside. A shiver shot through his body and he realised he didn't know where to go. Going from a warm kitchen out into the harsh elements was a shock. *Was it all a dream? What's happening to me?*

His thoughts spun out of control as he fought to make sense of where he was and what was happening to him. He remembered how he'd slipped and fallen earlier. Perhaps he'd been unconscious and only dreamt of the house and those conversations. *I must've hit my head hard. And yet…*

Oliver knew he had to focus on the urgent. 'Don't stay still,' he commanded himself. 'Go straight in any direction. Sooner or later you'll find something.' He hiked up a heath and journeyed along a line of trees to his left while looking about for signs of a road or a house.

After a few minutes, his chaotic thoughts began to calm and he tried to reflect with clarity both on what was happening and what was said. He was baffled by the events and the strangeness of his new acquaintances, but he couldn't ignore their stories— stories that, though outrageous and ancient, were somehow connected to his own.

Distractions often kept Oliver from life's big questions. But, out here all alone, he had nothing to do but walk and to think. As he did, a sense of forced isolation stabbed at him. His life was like a missing shoe or a singular plant growing on a water pipe: lonely, and somehow out of place. He realised his fears and addictions had divorced him from meaningful relationships. Yes, he could charm. But people often left his life as quickly as they came.

Soon, the wind softened and the clouds thinned out. He was still cold, but no longer shivering. He saw the stars emerge and moonlight made his path clearer.

Oliver wished he knew how to read the stars—at least which way was North or South. He supposed his grandpa would tease him for his ignorance of such a basic survival skill. Oliver smiled as he imagined the gruff Scotsman…

'Hey, city boy! Whatcha doin' out here?'

'Grandpa William? Wow! I've had such a strange night.'

'Ain't been drinkin' that London gin, have ye?'

'No! I'm a Scotch man—just like you taught me.'

'Good to hear. But there are far more important lessons I need to teach ye.'

'Like what? How to tell directions by the stars?'

'The stars could be a start. But there's far more to manhood than that.'

'So I've been told.'

'I know. I've been prayin' for ye.'

'This prayer stuff, it works?'

'Ye think I'm the type of fella that's into mindfulness? Of course, it works. It works cause God works.'

'I suppose, if I don't freeze to death, I should come up for another visit, eh?'

'Yer always welcome, lad.'

'I know. I'm just a bit scared.'

'What of?'

'Well, getting lost out here for one. But it's more than that. I'm afraid of who I am and who I'm becoming.'

'I'm listenin'.'

'Well, I know I've got some bad habits and that they'll have consequences.'

'It's good to hear ye realisin' that.'

'But it goes deeper than my habits.'

'Lemme guess: yer not what ye wanna be and far from who ye oughtta be. That it?'

'Yeah, Grandpa, you nailed it. But where does a man get the power to change who he is?' He continued for several more paces.

'Grandpa… Grandpa?' But all was silent. His question was unanswered.

35

OLIVER SHOOK HIS head. *The lack of sleep is messing with me. I'll ask my grandpa these questions for real one of these days—assuming I find my way out of here.*

As he came to the edge of the tree line on the heath, he looked left. What he saw caused him to pause and squint. In the moonlight, on the hill opposite him, he saw a silhouette of, what seemed to be, a pickup truck. *What's a parked truck doing way out here at this time of night?*

He turned towards the vehicle and began his march down the hill. When he reached the bottom, he could no longer see it and began his trudging up the next hill, rehearsing in his mind what he might say should he find anyone in the truck.

When he approached the top, the vehicle came back into view and was now able to see someone on its opposite side. 'Hello!' Oliver called.

The person appeared to be hunched over something Oliver couldn't quite make out and did not attempt to respond to his greeting. Oliver walked around the truck and approached, what now seemed to be, the backside of a man.

'Hello. Excuse me, I don't mean to startle you.'

The silhouette raised a hand. 'Hush!' a man's voice cried out.

'I-I... OK.' Oliver stood, not daring to come any closer. The moonlight, now to his right, allowed him to see that the man was staring down into a telescope.

The seconds that passed seemed like minutes as the cold breeze chewed into his now motionless body. Finally, the man stood up from the telescope and turned to Oliver. 'Sorry, when I'm star gazing I can't afford any distractions. What can I do for you?'

Oliver took another step closer to the man. He smacked his lips and said, 'Well, I saw your truck parked up here on the hill and I wanted to see what was going on.'

'You wandered up here at 2 am out of curiosity?' the man asked.

'I know that sounds ridiculous but, to be honest—'

'It's always good to be honest.'

'Um, yes, quite. Well, as it turns out, I was walking and now I seem to be lost.'

'Seem to?'

'OK, I *am* lost,' Oliver conceded. 'I don't know where I am or what direction I'm headed in.'

'Well, realising you're lost is the first step to finding your way. Where d'ya need to be?'

Oliver buried his hands in his pockets for warmth and took a deep breath. 'Well, when I began, I was headed to a manor house to meet some people. Now I don't know where I am. I'd ring them, but I can't get any signal out here.'

'That's a complaint I hear a lot. The city crowd doesn't seem to understand the value of escaping distractions.'

'You're from the country?'

'Not exactly. I grew up rural but was moved to the city as a teenage. Spent my whole adult life in the capital.'

'Me too. I grew up in North Hertfordshire but moved to London for my education. Hopefully, I'll find a job that will allow me to stay.' Oliver took a good look at the man. He was in his thirties and taller than Oliver. He had no beard, a bit of stubble, and wore a colourful flannel jacket.

'Come. Join me on the back of my pickup. I was about to take a coffee break anyway.'

Oliver followed him as he walked around the truck, opened its tailgate, and hopped up on it. 'Come and have a seat,' he invited.

Oliver jumped up next to the man and turned to look at the expanse before him. The valley was bathed in silver moonlight. His new acquaintance reached for a large thermos, opened it, and poured some steaming java into the lid. 'Wanna drink?'

'Yes, please,' Oliver said eagerly. Though the wind had died down, it was still cold and Oliver longed to wrap his fingers around something warm.

'Here, use my cup,' he said, pushing the thermos top into Oliver's hands. 'I'll drink out of the thermos. Just give it back. I'm particular about my cups.'

'Thanks,' Oliver replied, feeling more relaxed. He tightened his hold on the coffee—inhaling its lifegiving fumes.

'Besides the coffee, what else can I do for you?'

'I need a lift. Somewhere. Anywhere. Quaker Manor if you know where that is. If not, a petrol station or any place that's open. Somewhere I could get reception or send out a message.'

He nodded. 'Not a problem. I was just finishing up.'

'Really?' Oliver asked, pleasantly surprised. 'Thanks.'

The man took a chug from his thermos. 'Don't mention it. Just let me pack up my telescope and we can be on our way.'

And with that, the man hopped back down and walked around to his equipment.

'Do you need a hand?' Oliver asked.

'Nope. Just enjoy your coffee. Packing up a telescope properly is like life: you need good understanding if you're not gonna make a mess of it.'

'Oh, right. I gotcha.' Oliver said, still admiring the view.

'So, how exactly did you manage to get lost way out here in the middle of the night. You on some stag do weekend?'

'I came out for a school project but then my evening took an unexpected turn. Honestly, you wouldn't believe me if I told you.'

'Well, I know what it's like to not be believed. Sucks, really.'

'Do you come out here often to look at the stars?' Oliver asked, wanting to change the subject.

'Ha! Sounds like a pickup line.'

'Huh? Wait, no, I—'

'I'm only teasing you. But, to your question, yes, I've been gazing at the heavens since I was young.'

'A lifelong hobby, huh?'

'Yeah might call it that. Sometimes I feel as if these stars are my brothers.'

Oliver sipped the coffee, cherishing the hot liquid as it flowed into his cold body. The man came to the side of the truck and laid a box in the bed of the truck.

'Will that be safe back here?'

'I packed the box with memory foam. It's nuke proof.'

'Ah, gotcha,' Oliver said, sliding off the back.

'Hop in,' the man said, as he shut the tailgate. 'Let's get you to where you need to go.'

Oliver opened the passenger side door and climbed inside. The man entered and stabbed the keys into the ignition.

Oliver reached out his hand. 'Here's your thermos cup back.'

'Thanks for not stealing it.'

'No problem,' Oliver said with a chuckle. 'Well, I suppose if you're gonna give me a lift we should get acquainted. My name's Oliver.'

'Pleasure to meet you, Oliver. My name's Joe. Buckle up.'

'Nice to meet you, Joe.' Oliver said. Then, as he fastened his seat belt, it finally clicked. He froze.

Joe noticed. 'You OK?'

Oliver's lips parted, but words failed to come out. His eyes went clear and his face pale. He grabbed the door handle. His gut told him it wasn't a coincidence. Whatever was happening to him on this night hadn't come to an end. A moment of silence passed before Oliver released his grip on the handle.

'So, wi-will you continue the s-story?' Oliver asked quaking.

'Would you like me to?'

Oliver looked around. Did he have a choice? There was no one in sight. It was that or stay lost. But, if the night had taught him anything, it was that choices and their consequences are inevitable. This whole night had seemed a paradox of something both chosen and forced upon him at the same time.

Finally, Oliver nodded his head. 'Go ahead, Joseph.'

The Viceroy of Egypt shifted the truck into gear, released the clutch, and began to talk as the truck rolled forward into the night.

36

THE ASSUMPTIONS ABOUT my death were a bit exaggerated. True, premature death is what most slaves in the ancient world expected. But Heaven was with me.

I was seventeen when my brothers sold me to the traffickers. My new life was a complete shock. Judah was right when he said that, as a teenager, I hadn't been a hard worker. But a young man discovers a work ethic quickly when the whip of a lash hangs over his back and I soon lost my allergy to labour.

I was clever enough and had a gift for understanding how systems work. I advanced as much as a slave could but when my boss's wife lied and accused me of sexual assault, I lost what progress I'd made and ended up in prison.

I spent years in that prison and it was there my character was fashioned. My pride, impatience, love of comfort, and bitterness towards my brothers were all chiselled away by iron circumstances smashing against my life. Finally, Heaven lifted me out of the pit. I interpreted Pharaoh's dream and he was so impressed he made me Viceroy. He made it my job to prepare for the coming famine.

Once food shortages began, and people from outside Egypt flooded in to buy grain, I knew it was only a matter of time until my family came. I imagined what it would be like to see them again. But reflection failed to prepare me for their arrival.

I was sitting high above my administrators and soldiers. They were busy receiving money and distributing grain bags to the masses. Suddenly, there they were! The sight of them jabbed me in the gut. Rage, sorrow, shock, longing—all somersaulted inside of me. I knew I needed to act, but was unsure what to do.

So I threw them in prison. Ha! Every little brother's dream, right? Oh, don't look at me like that. After three days I knew that Heaven wouldn't be pleased if I left them there. Well, as Judah told you, they left and came back a year later.

When they returned, I ached to reveal myself to them, but I feared for my safety. I know, ridiculous, right? I could've had them all killed with a word. Yet, I was still their brother. Would they hate and envy me like they did when they were little?

So I laid a test for them using my full-blooded brother, Benjamin. It was then that I saw the change. Judah of all people, the brother most eager to get rid of me, sacrificed himself for my little brother. I couldn't believe he was the same man.

When Judah bowed before me, I had a choice to make. They had thrown me into a pit and separated me from my father! I spent thirteen years as a slave—and nine more in exile. They'd taken my life. Now I'd take theirs. That'd be justice!

Or would I?

I announced who I was. Judah was terrified. He was right to be. The others lost it too. They acted as if I were a ghost. And, after a fashion, I was. To say they were shocked would be a gross understatement. They were shaken to their core.

Then I told them the good news.

37

'GOOD NEWS? HA!' Oliver remarked as the truck rattled down a dark country road. 'I mean, I see how avenging yourself was good in a sense—good for you at least. But I bet they didn't see it that way.'

'No, the news was good for them as well.'

'How? Judah said he died—or a part of him died—at that moment. He never did explain what he meant. Did you imprison him? Torture him?'

Joe snickered as he stared forward out the windshield. 'I confess I found it amusing when Judah exploded with hysteria the moment I spoke to him in Hebrew. That was the little brother left in me. All my brothers went mental when I addressed them as me—thought I was a ghost.'

'How did you calm them down?'

'As I said, I spoke good news: their sins were forgiven.'

'So, you didn't dish out justice?'

'Justice is a word a lot of people throw around—as if they're qualified to distribute it. I used to be the same way as a youth, but I was no longer that man. The God of my fathers had exalted me to bring salvation. Not to condemn. He'd given me the authority to save lives, reconcile, and forgive—not to avenge myself on enemies. That day, I invited them into my kingdom.'

Cynicism burst from deep within Oliver. 'Just like that, huh? You guys lived happily ever after?'

If Oliver had meant to provoke, he failed. 'Was it hard to pardon them? Yes, I forgave them on that day—but I also needed to again and again after that.'

'I can't see why we should let people back into our lives who hurt us? Why should we forgive and trust abusers?'

'Forgiveness and trust are two different things.'

Oliver looked sceptical. 'How so?'

'I'll tell you in just a sec.' Joe looked over his shoulder and slowed the truck down as he pulled up along the side of the road and came to a stop. 'Hop on out. Follow me.'

Oliver looked around. He didn't see any manor—or anything else for that matter. 'Where are we going?'

'As I said, we're getting you to where you need to go. Come.'

Oliver hesitated. *I have no idea what this guy is—but what else am I gonna do? Stay in his truck?* Oliver climbed out and hurried to catch up with Joseph, now several meters ahead of him on a small dirt path that cut through an empty field.

'Your question is a good one—about forgiveness and trust. During my years in jail, Heaven taught me to forgive my brothers—and thus rescued me from the devouring cancer of bitterness. But it wasn't until I saw Judah offer himself for Benjamin that I knew they'd changed. Only when I saw that could I trust them again.'

'Did they stay trustworthy?'

'Mostly, yes. My biggest sorrow was that they doubted my sincerity. For years they wondered if I'd still seek revenge.'

Oliver worked to keep up with Joe's brisk pace. 'Were you ever tempted?'

'Every day!' Joe laughed. 'Well, not every day—but often. Less as time went on. I saw how Heaven used the treachery against me for good—for the saving of all Egypt. That softened me.'

'So God just lets us suffer so other people can benefit?'

'Suffering comes to everyone in this life regardless. Whether any good comes of it depends on how we respond.'

'Sounds like you and Judah both became saints before the end of your lives.'

'Heaven changed us both, that's true. I was the prince who forgave and Judah was the one who replaced a condemned man.

Heaven used both our lives to point to the One who was to come.'

'Huh? The One to come?'

'Surely you've heard about Him from your grandpa. He's the true forgiving Prince.'

A light went on in Oliver's head. 'Ah, yes. My grandpa told me. It seems all the stories point to Him in the end.'

'He's the great Replacement for us all.'

'The Replacement?'

'Most people spend their lives hoping not to be replaced by anyone who envies their career or their financial or relational success. The One who came, however, exchanged our failures with his success and died as our replacement.'

'I never thought about it like.'

'But that's not all. There's another part to his mission.'

'What's that?'

'I'm not sure you're ready to hear it.'

'C'mon. After tonight, I'm ready for anything.'

'Well, Ok. The One came so that you, Oliver, could die.'

And, with that, they walked out of the moonlight and into a deep darkness.

38

THEY STEPPED INTO a cluster of trees where the branches blocked out the light from the stars and moon. Oliver pulled out his phone and turned on its torchlight.

'Die?' Oliver groaned. 'Not this again. I thought, according to the story, the One came so that others could live.'

They walked through the shadows and came upon a pond with an old hut next to it. Joe stopped in front of its door.

'Yes. The One came so we could live. But the way to new life is through death. We only get one chance to die. In the life to come, we no longer have that opportunity.'

'Opportunity?' Oliver asked, shinning his torchlight and taking in his surroundings, 'How can you die before you die?'

'Our life is like a seed. If we hold onto it—fearing our seed might be replaced by nothing—it does just that, nothing. But, if we bury it, it produces life. Most people fear losing their life and so they tighten their grasp. If they were only to let it die in the ground, it would produce fruit.'

Joe's words made Oliver uncomfortable—not because he didn't understand them, but because he did. He wanted to change the subject. 'So, where are we?' he asked, glancing at the water. A wild goose, the type he might see in the Highlands where his grandfather lived, swam in circles in the pond. The hut was falling apart and its door was especially ugly.

'I told you I'd take you to where you needed to go.'

'Um, I said I was looking for Quaker Manor. I'd hoped you'd know the place—but would've been satisfied with a McDonalds or something if not. Whatever this hut might be, it's certainly not what I was looking for,' Oliver replied with irritation.

'This hut may not be where you expected to go, but it's where you need to go.'

Oliver glanced at the goose. It had stopped circling and was staring straight at him. He turned away from its gaze and towards the hut, now finding it even more horrific than before—like the places in movies where heroin addicts die or where paedophiles take kidnapped children to be molested.

Oliver fought to control his trembling. 'Listen, Joe, I don't know if you're an illness, a concussion, a paranormal creature— or even something other-dimensional from within a multi-verse. This whole evening seems to have siphoned off my sanity. But whatever you are, you have misunderstood something. What I am trying to do, what I have been trying all night to do, is just to meet with this band and get some footage so that I can make a trailer. What's before me, however, is an abandoned, wooden shack that looks like it stores dead bodies.'

Joe smiled kindly. 'You're here because your grandfather prays for you. Heaven sent us in response to bring you here.'

'But why here? And why on a night when I have such important plans? Will I fail school simply to learn that I'm crap with girls, fearful of risks, and lazy?'

'Tamar and Judah did right to point out your inner monsters. It's right that we face our darkness now. But we need more. We need to know where the darkness leads—and how to escape it. I'm here to show you Judgement Day.'

'Judgement Day? Isn't that what people face *after* death?'

'I'm offering you a short cut. Yes, you've already tasted judgment this evening, but I'm here to bring you to its final climax.

Oliver tensed. 'How exactly?'

'You'll see the future.'

'The future? As in, my future? I-I don't think I want to see that.'

'Don't you?'

'Well, before tonight, I would've. But, now, I'm not so sure.' Oliver glanced at the door again. It grew more horrid every minute. 'I might not like what I learn. What I've heard tonight has been difficult enough. Why would I want to face anything as terrible sounding as Judgement Day?'

'You are, at least, wise enough to hesitate. Wisdom comes with a cost.'

'Wisdom, huh?'

'Yes. Wisdom and insight—more precious than gold.'

'Through that door?'

'Potentially,' Joe replied.

'Oh, so it's "potentially" now?'

'Few people want a foretaste of Judgement Day in this life. But Heaven's judgment teaches us wisdom—but wisdom, including whatever you find beyond that door, must be acted upon.'

'OK, ya know, theoretically, If I did open and enter it, how would it work? Will we sit down and you tell me my future?'

'No. To you, it has been granted to see and hear.'

'See and hear?'

'Yes. Like one of those trailers, you're so eager to make. I want to show you a trailer of your Judgement Day.'

Oliver began to sweat. He glanced at the hut's door and turned back quickly. 'Do I have to go in to see? Could I just open the door and look in from the outside'

'You must enter.'

Oliver knew. Somehow, he'd known from the moment they'd arrived. Oliver stepped towards the door. With each advancing movement, his heart rate increased. The door was covered in splinters, the handle was rusty, and Oliver was certain he saw a couple of beetles crawling in and out of its cracks.

Yet, Oliver knew he needed whatever lay just behind that door—however terrifying and dark it may be. He looked down at his feet. 'OK,' he sighed. He turned off his phone's torchlight, slid it into his pocket, and wrapped his palm around the rusted metal.

He turned the handle. Gnashing his teeth, he pushed the door open and stepped into the utter darkness of his judgement.

39

THE MOMENT OLIVER stepped into the hut, liquid night whipped around and cocooned him in shadow. He covered his eyes and screamed. Then all went still. For a moment, he experienced a silence deeper and more profound than any he'd ever encountered.

Am I dead? he wondered. Then he heard his heart beating. *OK, I'm still alive. That's good. I think.*

He began to sense a dim but growing light from between his fingers. Slowly, he lowered his hands. When he opened his eyes, he sprang back. 'What the—?' Oliver gasped as an unexpected pillar of light stood in front of him.

It was a Christmas tree. Oliver was in the sitting room of a warm cottage decked out with fairy lights and holiday decorations. Christmas carols were playing in the background and the smell of mulled wine wafted in from the kitchen stove.

Presents piled under the tree and small, wooden Santas sat on the bookshelves. He was in the sitting room of a cottage that was warm, open, and felt of familial love.

'Huh, Judgment Day's not looking so bad.'

A beautiful young woman in a pyjama onesie suddenly entered the room with a book and a mug.

'Excuse me, sorry!' Oliver cried, afraid his presence would scare the girl.

But the girl walked right past him and sat on a large chair filled with cushions. She opened her book and began to read.

'Hello?' Oliver asked, but there was no response.

'She can neither see nor hear you,' a voice said from behind. Oliver turned. It was Joe in his colourful flannel.

'This isn't quite what I'd expected. If this is what the Universe judges I should get, I can't complain. I dig the cottage—and the girl, who's she? Please say she's my wife? She's beautiful. How far in the future am I? She looks to be my age now. Do I marry a younger gal when I'm older?'

'Watch and listen,' Joe replied.

Oliver heard voices approach and a middle-aged couple entered the room. The woman sat down on the settee facing the girl on the other side of a coffee table and the man walked into the kitchen.'

'Would you like something to drink, Anja?' the man asked. I'm getting your mum coffee.'

'No thanks,' the girl replied. 'I've got some mulled wine.'

'Are they her parents?' Oliver asked.

'They are,' Joe replied.

'Well, wait then, where am I? I can't be the dad—that guy looks nothing like me.'

Joe said nothing.

The man returned to the room with his wife's coffee and a newspaper. He sat next to her on the settee and began to read. The woman lifted her mug gently to her lips and looked about the room with wonder in her eyes as if she were seeing the decorations for the first time.

'Did you leave a shoe on the window sill?' the mother asked.

Anja looked up from her book. 'Of course, Mum. I'm certain I'll be on St.Nicholas' good list,' she said with a smile.

'Pffh. We'll see about that, young lady,' her mum replied with a wink. 'Help me make the Christmas breads later and perhaps Krampus won't throw you in his scary sack.'

'I thought Krampus put coal in my shoe if I was bad.'

'That's for mildly bad kids—the rotten ones get kidnapped.'

Anja smiled. 'Yes, I'll help make the breads tonight. I would've even without the threats of abduction,' she replied, and went back to her book.

The mother continued to look around the room.

The father interrupted the silence. 'Oh, my!'

'What is it honey?' the mother asked.

'It's, um, well. I'm not sure.' He handed her the newspaper. 'Have a look at this for yourself.'

The woman gazed into the newspaper for a moment.

'Everything OK?' the daughter asked.

'No!' the mother suddenly cried.

'Is it him?' the man asked.

'I don't see how it could be anyone else,' the mother said, with a look of exasperation. She held her hand to her chest and turned to bury her face in her husband's side. 'Oh, Max!' she exclaimed.

Oliver's eyes popped. 'Wait, no, it can't be. I know them! That's Max from school, just forty pounds heavier, and that's…' Oliver was unable to finish.

Joe spoke. 'Yes?'

'That's Elise. She's aged… but I can still see her young beauty in her older face. Why's she married to Max? That's awful!'

Joseph silently pointed back to the family.

Anja asked again. 'Guys, come on, what is it?'

Max placed his hand on the back of Elise's head and looked over at his daughter. 'It's someone we went to school with in London many years ago. Your mother knew him well.'

'What happened to him,' Anja asked. 'Was he a friend of yours?'

Elise pulled her face away from Max's chest. Mascara ran down her face as she reached for a tissue to blow her nose. She looked over at her daughter.

'He was a boy I kinda dated for a while. He's dead.'

40

'A BOY YOU dated died?' Anja inquired with concern.

'Well, it was never official, honey,' Elise replied. 'But we spent a lot of time together.'

'I'm so sorry, Mum.'

'Thank you, honey.'

'So, he wasn't a boyfriend?'

'Well, I waited for him to make a move. But he never did. Perhaps he never saw me as girlfriend material. I gave him time to decide but—'

'But he never did. And I, for one, am thankful for that.' Max interjected. 'Still, I'm sorry to hear that he died—especially in such an unfortunate way.'

The conversation Oliver was hearing yanked his gut into his throat. 'Me? Th-they're talking about me, aren't they?' he asked, almost vomiting his words. 'No, I can't be dead. How old are these people? Their forties? Fifty? I can't be dead before fifty!' Oliver shouted.

No one responded.

'How'd he die?' Anja asked gently.

'The newspaper says he, Oliver, died of head trauma after an accident in the shower,' Max responded soberly.

Elise shuddered and stared out the window. 'Tragic.'

'That's a strange way to die,' Anja remarked.

'It may sound unusual, but bathroom deaths are more common than you'd think. In Oliver's case though, it probably involved alcohol or drugs.'

'Was he an addict?'

'Not when I knew him,' Elise said mournfully. 'He was more determined than anyone I knew to be somebody significant in the film world. He had a couple of early successes, but then he made bad choices. He burned his bridges and the industry cut him off. He spent years trying to get back in with little success. He was disillusioned by it all and turned to drugs and heavy drinking to medicate his emotions .'

Max leaned forward. 'The last time we saw him, we were in London at a wedding reception for someone we all knew. Oliver showed up drunk—maybe high too, I dunno—and then got even more smashed while there.'

'I tried to speak with him,' Elise said, looking down, 'But that didn't go very well. He wasn't the same young man I once knew.'

'Sorry, Mum—such sad news on St. Nicholas Eve.'

'Thanks, darling. But the most tragic thing is not how he died—it's how he lived.'

'You mean being an addict?'

'Substance abuse was only the latest of his problems. When I met him, I hope your dad doesn't mind me saying this, he was unique, brilliant even. He'd written a beautiful script that was full of depth—one that moved me to tears. It was as if he saw what others were blind to. He was gifted.'

'He sounds special,' Anja noted.

'He was creative, I'll give him that,' Max nodded. 'But he was a boy that never grew up. Still, his death is tragic.'

'He was special,' Elise said, looking out the window with teary eyes. 'But he didn't have the character to carry his gift. I didn't understand why he made the choices he did. I thought it was laziness or procrastination. But now I realise he was afraid.'

'Afraid?' Anja asked. 'Afraid of what?'

'Afraid of failure, afraid of being replaced, afraid he wasn't man enough. He never married or had kids and his friendships were shallow. Talent without relationships will only get you so far. His existence revolved around making himself great. The more he fought to become a somebody, the more he became a nobody.'

Oliver fell to his knees. The lovely lips he'd longed to kiss were now pronouncing the final judgment over his life—and the verdict was more than he could bear.

The room and the people in it began to fade. The cosy smells and sounds of the cottage evaporated. A cold wind swept through the house and blew the warmth and beauty away. In their place, the trees came into view and Oliver found himself kneeling next to the pond.

He looked up at Joe. 'Is that my destiny?'

Joe stared back, saying nothing.

'Is that what my life will be? That can't be my fate!' Oliver cried, standing up as he did.

Joe said nothing.

'Speak, you stupid nightmare! Is that it? Will I spend my life trying to become a somebody but die a nobody?'

Joe spoke. 'The wreckage you saw is the ripening of all you chose in life.'

Oliver's hands shook. A tear ran down his cheek and his voice dropped into a whimper. 'This is me? Self-centred little me? I break Elise's heart—along with everything else?

'You hold your life so tightly that you can't give it to anyone or anything worthy of it.'

He walked over to Joe and bowed. 'What must I do? How do I escape becoming this man? How do I stop being me?'

Joe looked over at the pond.

Oliver tried to follow his gaze but felt as if he was wearing a concrete helmet. Something within him didn't want to look towards the water. Then, he felt an unexpected strength rise from inside that enabled him to turn towards it. The wild goose was still there, giving him a knowing look.

'That?'

'Yes, that.'

'Must I?'

'This is how the Universe works,' Joe responded.

Oliver walked to the pond's edge. He couldn't see through the water to the bottom. He picked up a handful of dirt and held it above the waters.

'I'm holding on too tight,' he sighed. 'I can't let go.'

'All Creation has the potential to be resurrected in the newness of life. But first, it must be buried with the One.'

Oliver's mind warred within him. 'My dreams of success, my victories—are all my good things my enemies?'

'You've worshipped angels as if they were gods. That's why they'll become your demons.'

Oliver understood. 'My life's all about gaining glory for myself. That's why I lose everything, right?'

Joe stared back.

Oliver knew it was true. Something within urged him to run away from the pond. His breathing grew heavy and his fists clenched at the thought of letting go.

'What if I lose it all?'

'In the end, you lose it all anyway,' Joe replied.

Oliver began to turn his head to look back towards the road from where they'd come. 'Could I—'

'I'll take you away from here and anywhere you ask—if that's what you want.'

Oliver stopped. He closed his eyes. He knew who he was and who he desired to be. There could be no going back. For this to work, Oliver Anderson had to die.

He sighed, 'Heaven help me.' And with that, he ran forward and threw himself into the depths of the pond.

41

THE DARK WATER swirled above Oliver, burying him for what seemed like an eternity. The moment he sank deep enough for his feet to hit the pond's bottom, he shot straight up into a blinding light.

The morning rays shot through the glass window. He clenched tightly to the leather book in his hands as he turned away from the sun's glare.

Slowly, he opened his eyes and took in his surroundings. Lights and cameras encircled him and an empty armchair sat across from the sofa he'd fallen asleep on.

'Judah!' Oliver called. 'Tamar! Joe!' But all he heard was the sound of his echo bouncing throughout the old house.

He put the Bible down and pulled the blanket off his lap. He stood, extended his arms, and stretched. He slapped himself to test if he was in a lucid dream.'

'Hello? Anyone?' he called again.

No one responded.

He walked over to the front door and opened it. The cold air rushed in upon him like a crashing wave, and his body tightened under its chill. A thin layer of snow whitened the hills and trees all across the front garden and into the horizon. He gazed at the rising sun and felt its rays on his skin. He stood still and enjoyed the peace of that moment more than he had enjoyed anything for a long time.

After soaking in the morning glory, he turned and walked to the kitchen. Even terrible coffee might taste good on a morning like this. He heated the kettle, filled his cup, and wandered back into the lounge room where he stared at the unused cameras and lights.

Out of habit, he picked up his phone. His eyes popped.

'Reception!' he said out loud. He also had dozens of new messages—all from two sources.

The first was the band. A shiver shot down his spine as he read them. They were at another manor—and had been going nuts all night trying to find him. They'd waited for him until after midnight. Only then did they pack up and return to Cardiff. *So I did spend the night in the wrong place. Could it have been more than a dream?*

The other messages were from Elise. She'd attempted to message him last night to confirm all was well and was frustrated her messages weren't coming through. The last message he received, however, was one she'd sent that very morning. 'OLIVER!' it read in all caps. 'YOU'RE IN THE WRONG HOUSE! ARE YOU OK? I'M COMING!!!!' with a few hysterical emojis to follow.

Oliver grimaced when he considered she'd been worried on his account. He shot off a reply. 'I'm OK. I think. Crazy night. Please don't inconvenience yourself. I've reception now. I'll call a taxi to get me and the stuff back to London. Enjoy your fam,'

He looked at the sky and wondered how he'd describe to the taxi service where he was. Now that he had a signal, perhaps he could get enough data to open his maps and give them a road name or a postcode. The reception was still meagre and it took an eternity—a full seventeen seconds—for his maps app to open. It showed him, not to his surprise, that he was in the middle of nowhere.

As he thought about what he'd tell the driver, he heard a distant rumbling. He looked out the window and smiled. He'd never been so happy to see vomit green in his life. It was Elise. He opened the door and walked into the cold.

When Elise's car stopped in front of the house, she leapt out, ran over to him, and threw her arms tightly around his body in the way every man dreams of his crush doing. When she did, he spilt some of his coffee onto the snow, but he didn't care. He wouldn't have cared if it was the best coffee in all London. She held him for seven seconds, but they were the seven most delicious seconds of his life.

She pulled back, slightly embarrassed. 'Ar-are you OK?'

Oliver grinned. 'I am now,' he said and took a second to look at her. He thought she looked good—he'd always thought that. Her fair, blond hair framed her smooth cheeks and her eyes drew you in like deep, blue pools. But the thing he loved the most, the thing you could see in her eyes and her face, was just how kind and considerate she was.

A barrage of questions exploded out of her delicate mouth. 'I was so worried when I found out. Did you sleep here last night? Did anyone show up? Did the owner find you? What'd you do?'

'Yes. Maybe or kind of. No. And, you wouldn't believe it.'

'Huh?'

Oliver's smile stretched to his eyeballs. 'Come on in!'

Elise walked into the parlour and looked around. 'Wow... this place! How'd you sleep in here?'

'I'm not sure I did sleep. Or, then again, maybe I did. A lot,' Oliver said, shrugging his shoulders. 'How'd you know I was alone out here?'

'I was worried when I never heard from you so I went on the Ebony Mane website and found a contact number. It seems I woke up the lead singer,' Elise said with a shy smile. 'He explained to me you never arrived. That's when I went online and looked up "Quaker Manor" and realised I'd left you at the wrong place. I was so afraid!'

Her tender concern humbled him. 'Elise, you shouldn't have. I was all set to ring a taxi.'

'Oh.'

'Not that I mind!' Oliver added quickly. 'In fact, I'm thrilled to see you.'

'Really?' She noted his sincerity, void of any plastic charm.

Oliver took a step closer and placed his hand on her arm. 'Very much so. I'm only sorry to inconvenience you. I won't offend you by offering you instant coffee from this kitchen. It's dirt. But I want to buy you a big breakfast after we leave here.'

Elise's face grew sceptical. 'You're taking me out for a meal and offering to pay?'

'It's St. Nicholas Day, right?'

'Yeah, but—'

'I know. I usually suck and you're right to be surprised.'

'Well, I wouldn't put it like that,' Elise said, not wanting to hurt his feelings.

'I would.'

'Do you want me to help you pack up the equipment?'

'Not yet. First, would you mind sitting with me for a moment? I'd like to tell you something.'

Elise hesitated. 'But, can't you tell me in the car?'

'I'd rather not tell you while you're driving—if that's ok. I want to look in your eyes when I say it.'

'Oliver, you're making me nervous now.'

'Please, trust me,' he said gently.

Elise felt the weightiness of his words. 'OK.'

She sat down with him on the dusty sofa. He reached over, took her hand in his, and looked into her sweet, rose and white face. He swallowed a knot in his throat and the words flew out.

'I'm sorry. I've bollixed up everything. I've failed to be a man; I've failed to make clear my feelings for you. I'm sorry about that. I'm also sorry for the way I've taken advantage of your kindness. You've helped me with far too many difficulties and I've helped you with far too few. It's been the most uneven friendship one could imagine. I'm sorry for not thinking more about what challenges you're facing. I never even asked you about your film project—all while you were driving me out here so I could get footage for mine!'

He continued, shaking his head and looking down. 'I'm sorry that you've bought me coffee the last gazillion times and I've never returned the favour. I know, I suck.

'Also,' he said with a shudder, 'I'm sorry I didn't tell you about the equipment. I lied and used you. When I die and go to hell, the demons will lock me in a screening room and make me watch that moment I loaded up your car with contraband over and over again for eternity. I should've never done it. I made you an accomplice to my stupidity.'

His words overwhelmed her. They rushed out so fast, Elise could barely take it all in. She didn't know Oliver was capable of such an apology. Her emotional defences went up, unsure if he was putting on an act.

Oliver saw the disbelief in her face. 'I understand that you might doubt me. If I were you, I'd be uncertain too.'

Elise took a deep breath. She was still shocked, but she appreciated his words. 'Thank you,' she managed to whisper.

'And, so you know, I'll tell the school I took the equipment.'

Her eyes filled with concern. 'Won't you get in trouble?'

'A bit. But I deserve it. It's still the right thing to do.'

'What about the competition?'

'Nothing to fear. I'll do my best with the time and equipment I've got. If I don't win this year, I'll own it. It was my procrastination that screwed it all up.'

'Don't you care?'

'I do. But there are other things I care about more,' Oliver said, smiling at her.

'Oliver Anderson? Are you ill?'

'I've wondered that myself more than once during the night,' Oliver said with a laugh. 'Listen, I don't mean to shock you by saying all this, but doesn't your faith teach you that people can change?'

'Yes, but—'

'Well, being alone here in the house all night has allowed me to—how shall I describe it?—to wrestle with some inner ghosts?'

'Ghosts?' Elise's eyes lit with curiosity. 'It sounds like you've had an interesting time. Can you tell me more over breakfast?'

'Of course. Let's load up the car.'

And with that, he leaned in and kissed her on the cheek. She blushed. He rubbed his thumb on her cheek and she lifted her hand to his head and her fingers ran into his hair.

Suddenly, her smile faded.

'Oliver?'

'Yeah?'

'Why's there lipstick on your forehead?'

EPILOGUE

STUDENTS FLOODED OUT of the building and onto the London streets. One girl stood amidst the flow of humanity and looked about in all directions.

'Boo!' said a voice from behind her.

'Oliver!' she exclaimed with a smile, throwing her arms around him. A second later she pushed him back and swatted his shoulder. 'You know I hate to be scared.'

'That's probably why I do it,' he said with his mischievous grin. 'How was your class?'

Elise's smile disappeared. 'Not so great.'

'No. What's the matter?'

'I'll tell you over coffee.'

'OK, no hints?'

'It's Ms. Jenkins. She's insisting I incorporate some MAGBT symbolism in the film. Says the production needs to reflect school values.'

'Oh, no. What are you gonna—'

'No, not here. I don't want to be overheard by other students. Let's go to an out of the way coffee house where we can talk freely.'

'As you wish, my lady,' Oliver replied with a bow. 'Let's go to Beans. I never see students there.' And off they dashed.

'Until we get there, tell me: how are you feeling about your big day?'

'Which one?' Oliver asked. 'My debut as your lead actor or my baptism?'

'Let's not talk about the film for now. Tell me about the baptism. You ready?'

'I think so. Just thinking through the family issues.'

'Which ones?'

'Well, your parents are Catholic. Do you think they'll be comfortable at our Baptist church?'

'Oliver, we've been through this. My parents freaked out when I started attending with you, but they've gotten over it. Now they're just glad I'm dating a Christian.'

'You think your mum's forgiven me for the weekend I spent at yours?'

'I told you, she found it funny—I think she even likes you. Just don't refer to her food as "perogis" again.'

'Gotcha. Well, she may like me, but she's over the moon proud of you.'

Elise blushed. 'Well, perhaps she thinks I'm all right.'

'All right? You won the film contest and are now overseeing the most expensive student production in the school's history. They gave you twice the budget they gave me last year, and no one saw it coming. You blew past Max, Adam—and me.'

She turned in front of him, stood up on her toes, and kissed Oliver on the lips. 'Sorry to replace you.'

He smiled. 'Can't think of anyone I'd rather be replaced by,' he whispered back. 'Anyway, didn't we agree not to talk about the film till we got to the coffee house?'

'Right, sorry. It's just so all-consuming! Back to your baptism: what else is bothering you?'

'My own family. Grandpa William is coming down from Scotland to do the baptism. He's old and doesn't do well with travel—plus he says he's allergic to England.

'And my mum and dad, well, they'll be there, but they're not Christians. Dad's already made at least one cynical comment. And mum, well, she'll love me whatever but still, I know she won't get it. Then there's my brother who—'

'Stop!' Elise interrupted with a laugh. 'Look at you! How many times do I need to tell my precious, overthinking worry-wart not to be afraid? God's in control. He'll take care of you.'

'You're right. I keep forgetting.'

'Not that I'm a perfect example. You'll hear plenty of my anxiety in just a minute.' She said as they approached Beans.

'Go have a seat. I'll order. You want the normal?'

'Actually, I'd like to try—'

But Elise was interrupted by Oliver's phone. He took it out of his pocket and looked at it. 'Huh?'

'What is it?'

'It's my dad.'

'Really? He never rings you.'

'I know.'

'Are you gonna answer it?'

'Yeah.' He poked his phone and put it to his ear.

'Hello? Dad?' Oliver listened for a moment. 'I'm getting coffee with Elise... No, I'm OK... What?' He stared into Elise's eyes. The expression on his face told her something was wrong. 'No! Is he all right?'

Elise's eyes lit with worry.

'Yes, dad... yeah, thanks for telling me... bye,' Oliver finished and hung up.

'What's wrong?' Elise asked. 'What's the matter?'

For a moment, Oliver shook his head in disbelief. 'It-it's my grandpa.'

'William?'

'Yes,' he muttered. He leaned back against the glass wall of the coffee house.

'Is-is he all right?'

'He's in the hospital,' Oliver managed to get out, sitting down on the bench. 'He's had a heart attack. A bad one. They're not sure he'll make it.' And, with that, he lifted his hands to his face.

Elise gasped. 'Oh my, oh Oliver! I'm so sorry.'

'Yeah,' he mumbled through his hands.

Elise wrapped her arms around him in a side hug and, for a moment, let her boyfriend absorb the shock of the moment.

Finally, Oliver looked up. 'I need to grab a train up there. I can't let him die without seeing him one last time.'

'Yes, of course,' Elise responded. 'When should we leave?'

'We?'

'If you'll let me.'

'You're in the middle of overseeing the release of a six-figure production!'

'Please, Oliver. I don't want you going alone up there.'

'But your cast will need you here.'

'You're the star performer! What if you need me?'

'We're done filming. I'm just an actor who has to show up at the debut and look pretty, remember?'

Elise smiled tenderly. 'Oliver, I know I have big responsibilities here. But you're my priority. I know how much you love your grandpa. If he does pass away, I want to be with and comfort you. Plus, I don't want to lose what could be my last opportunity to meet him. Please let me go.'

For a moment, Oliver was speechless. 'Wow. You know I don't deserve you, right?'

'I know you'd do the same. Plus, I can work on the production remotely when I need to.'

'I love you. Truly.'

Elise blushed. 'Plus, I need to tell you about that MAGBT stuff. I don't know what to do—I'll wait until we get on the train. Do I have time to head back to my apartment and pack?'

Oliver nodded. 'Of course. I need to do the same. Let's aim to meet at the station in 90 minutes. That enough time for you?'

'Yeah, I can do that.'

'See you there.'

To be continued in…

Samson and the Siren

The third and final of the Oliver Anderson Trilogy

'SO, THE LAW has caught up with our infamous rebel.'

'Achish, my man! It's been a while.'

'I hope your new accommodations are to your liking.'

'Let's see: damp, smelly, crawling with insects, stinks. Yes, I'd say it's Philistine décor at its finest. I'm just a bit disappointed you haven't greeted me with a kiss.'

The General pressed his lips and smiled. 'Hm. Even now you're defiant. Remarkable.'

'Know what they say: old habits die slowly.'

'As will you.'

'Oo, Touché, Achish.'

'I see you've acquired some bruises,' the general said, poking the prisoner with his staff. 'I hope the soldiers weren't unnecessarily rough.'

'Gentle as maids.'

'And yet, this time you didn't get away?'

'And miss out on all this? You've gone all out for me.'

'Only our best for the Hebrew champion. Are the ropes too tight?'

'Well, if you'd come over and loosen them, we could have a cuddle.'

'Another time, perhaps. Anyway, you've had far more cuddles than you deserve lately.'

'Now what's that—'

'Fool!' the general interrupted. 'You're not the first man to have his downfall at the hands of a woman. Though, I confess, I've never enjoyed watching it happen this much. Ha! Struggling for words? You don't think she ever cared for you, do you?'

The prisoner bit his lip. 'I think you're jealous, big guy.'

'Jealous? What could a Philistine general ever envy in a Hebrew dog.'

'Because I had her.'

'You had nothing. She played you. And, in any case, tonight she'll be in my bed while you play with yourself in here.'

'What can I say? You two deserve each other.'

'We'll laugh at your expense before making love.'

'You know what they say about sloppy seconds, Achish.'

'Shut up! You'll suffer for your defiance.'

'Suffer, shut-up, uh-huh. Listen Achish, why don't you come back when you're ready to have, like, an adult conversation?'

'Slave!'

'You're losing your cool, General. You need to just sit down and calm—'

'No! You are weak as any man now. Your magic no longer works. You cannot back up your cavalier words with might.'

'OK—so I've had better days.'

'Ah, but they will only be getting worse, you see.'

'Promises, promises.'

'Do you like your new haircut?' the general asked, placing his hand on the prisoners bald head. He turned away. 'Oh? Nothing clever to say now? Do you think your hair is the only thing we'll be taking?'

'Well, I could shed a few pounds. All the crappy Philistine food your whore cooked for me has as added some weight.'

The general gritted his teeth. 'Your words will cost you, Samson. Guards! Get the pokers for his eyes. And do it slowly.'

Dear Reader,

Thank you for reading this retelling of Judah and Tamar. It's my sincere hope and prayer that the Oliver Anderson trilogy will create in you a deeper appreciation for the Biblical narrative and how God works in families and history to redeem us. If you are unaware, you may what to check Jesus' genealogy in Matthew 1. As it turns out, Judah and Tamar, and the crazy story of Genesis 38, is part of Jesus' family tree.

Could I ask you for a favour? If you've enjoyed this book, would you please leave a review on Amazon or share it on social media? Independent authors depend heavily on positive Amazon reviews.

Happy to hear from you at Read@JoshuaDJones.com. Thanks for reading,

Joshua

The Oliver Anderson Trilogy

Girl and the Guardian - The Genesis Ghosts - Samson and the Siren

(Mordecai & Esther) – (Judah & Tamar) – (Samson & Delilah)

Ingram Content Group UK Ltd.
Milton Keynes UK
UKHW041112300323
419409UK00021B/596/J